YIELD TO A TRAITOR

It is 1645 and the Civil War is raging. Rosalind Pendrill finds her Royalist loyalties severely tested when Roundhead troopers, under the command of Major Francis Latimer, are billeted in her home, Pendrill Manor. Rosalind should regard Francis as an enemy, but finds herself increasingly attracted to him. Her emotions are in further turmoil when her brother, Thomas, is taken prisoner by Francis and his troopers. To obtain her brother's freedom, Francis stipulates she must marry him . . .

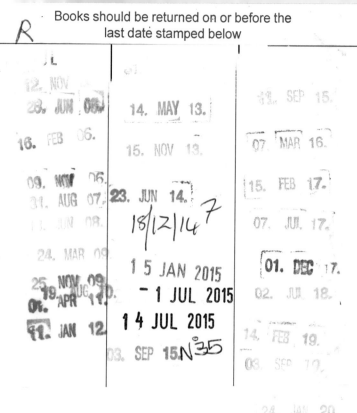

LINDA JAMES

YIELD TO
A TRAITOR

Complete and Unabridged

LINFORD
Leicester

First published in Great Britain in 2003

First Linford Edition
published 2004

British Library CIP Data

James, Linda
   Yield to a trait James, Linda
   Linford roman
   1. Great Britain Yield to a
   1642 – 1649 — traitor / Linda
   3. Large type b James
   I. Title   ROM LP
   823.9'2 [F]

   ISBN 1–84395- 1574071

Published by
F. A. Thorpe (Publishing)
Anstey, Leicestershire

Set by Words & Graphics Ltd.
Anstey, Leicestershire
Printed and bound in Great Britain by
T. J. International Ltd., Padstow, Cornwall

1

Rosalind struggled to free her mind from the last vestiges of sleep and opened her eyes to see her maidservant bending over her.

'Wake up, mistress, for pity's sake!' Mary cried, the flickering light from the candle she held concealing nothing of the fear in her anxious gaze.

'Whatever's the matter?'

Rosalind sat up and shivered as the chill air enveloped her body.

'Roundhead troopers, mistress! They burst in when William opened the door! Nathaniel Black is with 'em.'

Her glance slid nervously towards the door.

'He ordered me to wake you at once!'

Rosalind swung her legs out of bed and pushed her feet into soft slippers, while Mary helped her into a woollen robe. Nathaniel Black, here in her home! Her mind was seized by dread. Had he discovered she was hiding a Royalist?

Her worst fears were realised when she peered over the gallery rail and saw the Parliamentary soldiers positioned around the hall. Others were ascending the stairs and brushed past her, giving but a cursory glance at her long, unbound hair and night attire. Anger coursed through her, banishing for the moment her fear of their intrusion into her home.

Nathaniel was seated at the long, oak table, in the process of helping himself to a measure of her best claret. She had been acquainted with him for many years, but as she made her way down and encountered his cold, dark gaze, she realised his past friendship with her family would count for nothing. His assessment of her was chilling, but she was determined he would not see her fear. She halted at the end of the table and stared at him, a blazing light in her eyes.

'What explanation do you have, Master Black, for invading my home in this atrocious manner and at this late hour?'

His penetrating stare seemed to go right through her robe and she self-consciously pulled the edges closer together. He was not an unhandsome man, but there was something in his deep-set black eyes that always gave her the feeling he could read her mind.

'I do not need to explain my actions to you, Mistress Pendrill. You appear to have forgotten this is a time of civil war. I am here because I believe you are harbouring a traitor within these walls.'

'Then you believe wrongly, sir,' she answered, her voice trembling with fear and anger. 'What makes a traitor? Supporting our lawful sovereign or making rebellion and war as Parliament is doing?'

'Do not bandy words with me, mistress. Your pretended innocence does not deceive me. Over the last few weeks there has been a constant watch on your activities. You appear to entertain guests who spend an overlong stay in your home. They are not seen leaving, so where do they go, I wonder. My aim is to flush them out of their hiding place.'

'I wish you well in your task, Master Black, but you will find no-one to flush out.'

Nathaniel's gaze swept the length of her body with a possessive look in his dark eyes that filled her with new dread. She prayed the dim candlelight hid the revulsion she felt for him and his actions. She realised now how careless she had been. The Parliamentary authorities must have known all these weeks that she was sheltering fugitive Royalists. Were they also aware that the man she was hiding at this moment was far more important to the Royalist cause than any she'd helped previously? Why else would they burst into the manor so late at night?

The man they sought was hiding even now in the cellars. Sir John Verney was a close aide of King Charles and he carried dispatches from His Majesty, intended for Sir Edward Walker, the king's secretary. It was vital that more arms and fighting men were quickly assembled if the Royalist cause was to succeed against Parliament's forces. Seeing them in action, ransacking her home with ruthless efficiency, she realised Cromwell's army was no longer to be viewed with jeering contempt.

Rosalind's dislike for Nathaniel stemmed from the time he was lawyer to her late father. It wasn't just the fact he was a strict Puritan, it was the way his eyes lingered upon her whenever she was in the same room with him.

'Why do you persist in this foolishness, Rosalind? Do you not fear for your safety?'

He let out a sigh of exasperation.

'We know John Verney is hiding in this house. He was followed here from Lockstone Hall several hours ago. You can be assured we will ferret him out, with or without your help.'

'Be assured there will be no help from me, Master Black. If he were hiding here, do you think I would betray a King's man? Sooner my own life forfeit than that!'

'Your life may well be forfeit if you dabble in dangerous games, Rosalind,' he said quietly, but there was underlying menace in his voice.

In the upper rooms, it was evident the troopers had begun their thorough work of searching. Rosalind was thankful she had hid Sir John in the cellars and not in the secret room. At least there was an escape route through the cellars into an old underground tunnel which led to the fountain in the rose garden, but she knew the troopers would soon be demanding access to the cellars and she had to think of a way to warn Sir John and help him escape.

'Do you intend to destroy my house in your attempt to find the man you seek? Those louts up there seem to be well on the way to doing so!'

She tried to suppress the panic in her

voice, but Nathaniel sensed her agitation and satisfaction made him smile.

'No, my dear girl, Pendrill Manor will not be destroyed. The troopers have orders to go carefully. I have other plans for this house.'

He gazed around the hall with a possessive look which alarmed her. Surely he did not think he could be master here. Her father had died recently, but there was still her brother, Thomas, who would inherit the estate. He was away fighting with Prince Rupert's regiment. Could she stand up to Nathaniel Black alone?

A movement on the landing above caused Rosalind to glance up. It was Mary, held in the grip of a burly trooper. She looked terrified. It was then an idea came to Rosalind.

'May I return to my bedchamber?' she asked. 'I am feeling chilled and wish my maid to attend me.'

Nathaniel's eyes lowered to Rosalind's hands, holding together the edges of her robe.

'Very well, you may go, but remember, no tricks. There will be a guard outside your door at all times. Needless to say, I do not trust you.'

His words echoed in her head as she climbed the stairs.

'Release my maid,' she ordered. 'I have permission from Master Black to be allowed to go to my chamber and have her attend me.'

The trooper gave a derisive snort, but he loosened his grip and allowed Mary to follow her mistress. Once in the bedchamber, Rosalind locked the door and began to disrobe.

'Why are the Roundheads here, mistress? What do they want with us?'

'No time for questions now, Mary. Take off your gown, quickly, and slip my nightgown on. I will wear your clothes and go to warn Sir John. He cannot find the escape route alone.'

'Let me warn Sir John,' Mary offered. 'It's too dangerous for you. It would not matter if I got caught.'

'Nonsense! The danger to you would

be just as great,' Rosalind replied, slipping the brown serge gown over her head. 'I know exactly where Sir John is and it is my responsibility that he is here in the first place. Now get into bed. I will try not to be too long.'

Rosalind made certain her hair was hidden under the maid's white cap before she crept on to the landing and nearly jumped out of her skin when a trooper emerged from the shadows.

'What are you up to, girl?' he questioned suspiciously.

She turned, frustrated by the delay.

'I'm not up to anything. My mistress is so shocked by your brutish invasion of her home, she needs a hot posset to calm her,' she answered, hoping her imitation of Mary's country dialect sounded genuine.

'Go your way then and be quick about it.'

The trooper's tone was less severe, and once out of his sight, Rosalind sped down the back stairs as fast as she could. At the bottom she halted, hearing voices near at hand. She quickly hid herself in a dark corner before two troopers appeared, making their way to the kitchen. Her heart was thumping so hard she felt sure they would hear it. When they were gone, she hastened along the passage to the cellar door. With shaking hands she unlocked it with the keys she alone kept and stepped into the blackness.

High on a shelf there was a tinderbox. Her fingers felt along the ledge, eventually closing over the cold metal. She fumbled for several minutes, trying to get a spark to light her candle. At last a yellow flame spurted into life and feeling comforted by the flickering light, she began to make her way through the musty-smelling cellars that criss-crossed under the manor.

When she reached the area where she had tried to make John Verney as comfortable as possible with pallets on the floor, she called out his name. He didn't answer. It was so easy for a stranger to become lost in the warren of passages. She moved farther on, agitated by the thought they had so little time before the troopers might burst their way into the cellars. Suddenly, a tall figure loomed out of the blackness carrying a candle. She almost dropped her own in fright at his sudden appearance.

'Forgive me, Mistress Pendrill. I've startled you. I've been looking for the flight of steps which leads to the garden, but I fear I was losing my . . . '

He stopped speaking, seeing the anxiety causing her face to appear white and drawn in the dim light.

'You must leave here this instant, Sir John! The Roundheads followed you from Lockstone Hall. They were waiting to capture you as you left, but I fear their patience has worn out. I believe they will turn their attention to the cellars at any moment!'

John's hand went to the hilt of his sword in an unconscious gesture.

'I heard footsteps thudding about up there. That is the reason I tried to find my way out. They mustn't know of your involvement in this.'

'They already know I've been hiding Royalists, sir. Come, we have no time to lose!'

John followed her slight figure as they hurried through the narrow tunnels. They came to a flight of stone steps ascending into darkness. Rosalind went first and had difficulty pushing up the iron grill fixed into the roof. John took over and he eventually succeeded in dislodging the grill. He lifted his head above ground level to peer around the moonlit garden.

'I'll take my leave of you now, mistress.'

Rosalind caught hold of his sleeve.

'I will accompany you, sir. There is no possibility of recovering your own horse from the stable and you will not get far without one. I know where you can obtain a horse at Ned Holden's smithy, not far from here.'

'You have involved yourself enough, Mistress Pendrill. Direct me to Master

Holden's and I need trouble you no further.'

'I am familiar with the area and can guide you there swiftly,' she replied, snuffing out the candle and easing herself past him on to the base of the fountain floor.

John Verney had no choice but to follow and together they heaved the iron grill back into place.

'You are a very determined and courageous young woman,' John said in low tones as they hurried towards the orchard.

'It is the least I can do, sir. I know how important your errand is for the cause.'

As they reached the shelter of the orchard trees, they heard the distant shouts of the troopers spilling into the grounds. Another minute and they would not have been able to use the escape route without being seen. At the farthest end of the orchard was a gap in the hedge, large enough to squeeze through. Before them lay an open field.

'There is no cover until we reach the other side,' Rosalind said. 'Can you run across without stopping, sir?'

John grasped her hand.

'My legs are getting old, mistress, but for the King's cause they will do the best they can.'

The long grass and wild flowers of the meadow dipped and swayed in the breeze like a ghostly silver sea. By the time they had reached the other side, Rosalind felt a stabbing pain in her side.

'You must not go any farther, my dear,' John said, anxious for her welfare. 'I will find my way from here.'

'Give me one minute and I will be fine. I have come this far. I am not turning back now.'

The determination in her voice made him realise that whatever he said would make little difference to persuade this young woman to leave him.

'Very well, if that is your wish. If you are sufficiently rested we will go on.'

Tall hedges flanked the path leading to Ned Holden's cottage, towering over them like black sentinels. At last the outline of Ned's cottage came into view. All was in darkness. John pounded on the sturdy door until a flickering yellow patch of light appeared at one of the upper windows. The casement was opened and the pale blur of a face stared down.

'Who is it? What do ye want at this ungodly hour?' he shouted down.

'Ned, it is Rosalind Pendrill. I have a friend who needs your help!'

The blacksmith needed no second bidding when he heard Rosalind.

'One minute, Mistress Rosalind. I'll be down as quick as I can.'

Within moments, Ned opened the door and ushered them inside.

'This is Sir John Verney, Ned. He has important documents which must reach His Majesty's secretary. I have been hiding him at the manor, but a short while ago a troop of Cromwell's Ironsides stormed in, searching for him.

Have you a spare horse for Sir John?'

Ned turned to John.

'Yes, sir. I have a swift, sturdy mount for thee.'

'Good man, Ned. It is imperative these despatches reach their destination quickly.'

John took some coins from a pouch at his belt and gave them to Ned.

'I would willingly help thee for nothing, sir, but horses are hard to come by lately. The price has rocketed since the war began. Follow me to the stable, sir.'

Rosalind was about to follow the two men, but John turned to her.

'Stay here in the warmth, mistress. You have done your task well and we will part company here. One day, God willing, you will be rewarded for your faithfulness and bravery.'

He lifted her hand to his lips.

'I seek no reward, sir,' she replied, 'other than knowing you complete your mission safely.'

'I am forever in your debt, Mistress

16

Pendrill. Let us hope we meet again in happier times.'

He gave her one last smile before moving to the door and following Ned into the yard. Some minutes later, Ned returned and eyed Rosalind with fatherly concern.

'How about a hot posset before ye head back to the manor, mistress?'

'Thank you, Ned, but I must make haste and return before I am missed. Nathaniel Black came with the troopers. He is an agent for Parliament's forces and if he discovered I had deceived him, I shudder to think what he will do!'

Ned swore under his breath.

'Pardon, mistress, but I never liked that sanctimonious Puritan. Now, if thee is ready, I'll see thee safe home.'

Rosalind was grateful for his company as they walked along the pitch dark lane, with only a lone owl calling out to break the silence. When they reached the meadow, she turned to Ned.

'I go on alone, Ned. God bless you for all you have done this night.'

Ned was reluctant to let her go on without him, but he finally relented under Rosalind's pressure for him to return home. Even so he remained at the edge of the field until he could no longer distinguish her slight figure hurrying through the long grass.

Now she was alone, fear began to prickle along Rosalind's spine. The trees in the orchard loomed ahead, ghostly shapes swaying against the moonlit sky. She squeezed through the gap in the hedge and halted. A twig had snapped underfoot! There was someone hiding among the trees! Her whole body became alert for the slightest sound or movement. It did not prepare her, however, for the several figures emerging from the darkness and advancing towards her. She hesitated only a second before catching up her long skirts and taking to her heels.

'Stop! In the name of Parliament!'

The crisp command shattered the

night air, but Rosalind had no intention of stopping. Her only thought was to gain the sanctuary of her bedchamber and discard Mary's clothing before her true identity was discovered. Faster and faster she ran, through the dense apple trees, on through the rose garden, past the fountain as if the Devil himself was after her!

The troopers were catching up and she turned her head to see how far away they were. It was her undoing. She tripped over her own feet and fell to the ground. The impact knocked the breath from her body. She was struggling to her feet when iron hard hands gripped her upper arms and hauled her into an upright position.

'Meeting your lover, my beauty, or up to more dangerous games, eh?' the trooper said close to her ear.

'I do not have to explain my actions to you, you big brute.'

She struggled against his superior strength.

'Think yourself some kind of lady, do

yer?' he sneered.

Rosalind realised with dismay she'd forgotten to speak in the country dialect.

'You'll have to explain your actions to Master Black, my girl. I'm sure he'll be interested in our midnight jaunt. Come on!'

He began to haul her towards the house. There was no way she could bluff her way out of this predicament. She could only hope it was not all in vain and John Verney reached his destination.

Nathaniel was in the parlour, standing with his back to the fire when Rosalind was unceremoniously pushed into the room. He stared at her, a puzzled frown on his forehead. Then recognition came and his expression turned to fury.

2

Nathaniel snatched the cap from Rosalind's head and she winced in pain as his fingers caught in her hair. She seemed unafraid and raised her head to meet his gaze with defiance in her eyes.

'There is no need for further pretence.'

His gaze ran with contempt over her rough, serge gown.

'I know it is for John Verney's sake you entered into this charade. Why do you place yourself in such danger for a cause already lost? It is only a matter of time before we capture him, then all this will have been in vain!'

'Were the cause lost a thousand times over, I would still risk my life for the King.'

Her quietly-spoken support for King Charles brought a wry twist to Nathaniel's lips.

'I have warned you that if you meddle in men's affairs you must suffer the consequences and that could mean losing your life!'

He took hold of her shoulders and she could feel his frustration in the tightness of his fingers digging into her soft flesh.

'Forget your high ideals, Rosalind,' he urged. 'You are young and beautiful. Your thoughts should be of marriage, not of a mad sovereign who has plunged the country into civil war.'

He sighed in exasperation when she remained silent.

'You leave me no choice. I am seizing this manor and its lands in the name and by the authority of Parliament.'

'Sequester the manor!' she exclaimed. 'You have no lawful right to take such action!'

He moved to the table and poured wine into two goblets, oblivious to the horror on her face. He offered her the wine, but she declined.

'Open your eyes to reality, my dear.

The King can show only token resistance now. He hasn't the arms or the fighting men to defeat Parliament. We are gaining the upper hand in almost every campaign, thanks to the military genius of men such as Fairfax and Cromwell. With the addition of the New Model Army we will be invincible.'

Rosalind wanted to scream at him that it was all untrue, but she knew since the battle of Marston Moor, the year before, the royalist cause was going disastrously wrong. Nathaniel interrupted her thoughts.

'I shall reside here at the manor to ensure your activities do not continue. Pendrill Manor will never again be used to hide Royalists.'

'I think sequestration is but an excuse. You have coveted this house for many years, is that not so?' she asked boldly.

His eyes narrowed at her bluntness.

'You do me an injustice if you believe my sole aim is to usurp your brother from his rightful position. My only concern is for you, my dear. Is it not more favourable that I take control rather than some unknown person?'

'I care nothing for your concern, neither do I recognise or accept your assumption that you can walk in here and assume the rôle of master.'

She was past caring that her forthright manner might goad him to further anger as she continued.

'Does loyalty mean so little to you that you now regard as enemies those you once looked on as family?'

Nathaniel appeared unruffled by her tirade.

'A civil war divides where it will, irrespective of loyalties. Do not imagine reference to how matters were before this conflict will make me more lenient.'

'I am well aware that is an impossibility,' she answered with contempt in her tone. 'What do you intend to do now?'

He studied her for a moment.

'What would you have me do,

Rosalind? My duty is to inform the authorities and let them decide an appropriate punishment.'

'Then you dare do no other than your duty,' she replied in a quiet voice.

'Give me your promise you will never again become involved in politics and I will allow this matter to go no further,' he suddenly decided.

'I cannot make that promise, Nathaniel.'

He was perplexed.

'Are you so stupid that the lives of a few stray cavaliers mean more to you than your own life? If this ever happens again I cannot vouch for your welfare, do you understand?'

'I understand perfectly, but I cannot say I will never help my friends given the opportunity.'

'You have always been stubborn and wilful, Rosalind. Beware it does not bring about your downfall one day.'

'Do you not fear my brother's anger, Nathaniel?'

'Why should I fear Thomas Pendrill?

He is nothing but a young, arrogant pup,' he said scornfully.

'Thomas will surely seek your death for placing so much as one foot on our land.'

'Your brother is more than likely dead!'

His statement was shockingly blunt.

'I received a report some days ago that Thomas Pendrill was one of several Royalists involved in a skirmish at Siddlesham. It appears they were all killed trying to escape from an inn where they were hiding.'

Rosalind felt the room begin to revolve as his words sank in. He put an arm around her shoulders and led her to the settle by the fireplace. This time she did not refuse the wine he offered and she sipped the sweet liquid gratefully. She had no cause to doubt his statement that Thomas was dead, but she was too numb to consider the implications if it was true. To whom could she turn now? Her only other relatives lived many miles away in

Yorkshire and were on the side of Parliament.

'If it is as you say and Thomas never returns, this manor is mine by birth-right and I will oppose your claim every inch of the way. A Pendrill does not yield anything without a fight and we never yield to traitors!'

He chuckled in amusement, his bold gaze sliding over her figure.

'As you appear to be the last of the Pendrills, I might find the prospect of a fight with you rather pleasing. I am inclined to think my stay here will be most pleasurable.'

His words carried a meaning that Rosalind could not mistake. She swore silently if he attempted to touch her she would defend herself with all the strength she possessed.

'Shortly I expect a further troop of horses to arrive here to swell the number of our forces already in this area. The officer in charge, Major Latimer, is determined to subdue once and for all any remaining pockets of resistance. I know the man and his resolve. When they do arrive I hope you will extend the hand of welcome to him and ensure the troopers are accommodated adequately.'

She lifted her head to meet his penetrating gaze.

'The forces of treason are not welcome in this household. I will make it plain to Major Latimer that he and his men are here without my consent. As for accommodation, the rooms above the stables will suffice for them!'

Nathaniel took note of the stubborn set to her mouth and deemed it wise not to goad her further. She would realise in time to rail against the presence of the military at the manor was futile. His gaze rested on the heavy abundance of her hair. He suddenly had the urge to touch the silken tresses, but he restrained his hand. He did not wish to alarm her too soon. His chance would come if he was patient.

'You may go to your bedchamber, Rosalind. You need time to reflect on the change in this household and its effect upon yourself.'

Rosalind was only too pleased to leave Nathaniel's presence and return to her bedchamber. Mary was in a highly-nervous state and full of questions, but Rosalind dismissed her, saying she would tell her everything in the morning. She quickly took off the serge gown and handed it to her. When the maid had dressed and left the room, Rosalind sank into her bed, physically and emotionally drained after her encounter with Nathaniel.

She knew she had escaped his wrath lightly, but did he have an ulterior motive for not reporting her involvement in helping Royalists? It was clear where his ambitions lay and she realised his allegiance to Parliament was the tool by which he gained control of the manor. What else would he covet, she wondered, as she drifted off into an uneasy sleep.

Rosalind was wondering which gown to wear for the coming day ahead, when she heard a commotion in the courtyard below. She left off her contemplation of her attire and hurried to the window, afraid John Verney may have been captured after all. There was no sign of him, she noted with relief, but what she did see brought dread to her heart. A troop of soldiers was arriving, presumably the one Nathaniel had warned was to bolster the already strong Parliamentary force in the area.

She watched in dismay as their horses ploughed through the hens and geese that always strutted around the courtyard in total freedom. She was so incensed by the thoughtless behaviour of the soldiers, it took her a moment to realise some of the men had seen her scantily-clad figure and began calling to her. The bawdy comments were heard by their officer, dismounting near the main entrance. The next minute he was striding across the courtyard issuing orders in a furiously cold voice. Silenced by the anger in his tone, the men began to move away towards the stable.

Rosalind knew she should move from the window, but her feet felt as if they were fastened to the floor. Even though she was acutely embarrassed, she couldn't tear her eyes away from the officer, who was staring up at her with keen scrutiny. His gaze slid to the thin chemise she was wearing and an expression of contempt crossed his dark features.

With great effort, Rosalind tore her gaze from his and closed the casement with some force. It was obvious what he thought of her and her cheeks burned with humiliation. Then a wave of defiance rose within her. This was her home. She could not prevent them taking possession, but she could be as irritating as possible to these traitors.

She chose to wear a dark blue velvet gown. The neckline was low for the daytime and she covered her shoulders with a wide collar made of finely-worked ivory lace. Mary pinned up her hair into a knot near the crown of her head and left ringlets hanging on either side of her face. When she was ready she took a deep breath to quell the churning in her stomach. Being defiant towards Nathaniel was one thing, but she had heard Roundhead soldiers could be brutal and she was alone, with no-one to give her aid.

She began to descend the stairs, but halted midway and stared with indignation at a trooper who was in the process of taking anything of value he could find in the hall and placing the items in a sack. Two pairs of silver candlesticks, which had taken pride of place for many years on the long dining table, were disappearing into the sack when Rosalind dared to question his actions.

'What are you doing? Those items are my property!' she called.

The trooper gave a mere glance in her direction and continued to fill the sack. Rosalind hurried to him, her heart thumping in anger and fear. She grasped his arm in an attempt to stop him.

'Keep out of my way, wench. I have orders to follow!' he snarled, knocking her arm away.

'Please return those items to where they belong or your commander shall hear of this!'

The trooper ignored her and lifted the sack over his shoulder.

'These fine things will help us win the war, little lady.'

'So you resort to stealing to win the war, do you?' she scoffed. 'Brutality and theft is typical of Cromwell's Ironsides.'

The trooper dropped the sack to the floor. He moved towards her and reached out to grip the soft flesh of her upper arms. His gaze travelled down the rich material of her gown.

'What do yer know of Cromwell's Ironsides?' he sneered. 'Very little, I should think. I reckon yer know nothing of real life and how the poor have to live. Or do yer even care?'

His contemptuous statement stung

Rosalind. She was about to answer his assumption that she cared nothing for the poor when he suddenly pulled her close to him.

'No answer, eh? Lost for fancy words?'

He leered down into her face.

'Shall I show yer what we do to female malignants?'

He pressed his mouth forcefully against her own and she was powerless to prevent him as he held her arms in a vice-like grip. Neither of them heard someone enter the hall.

'Simmons! Release that woman!'

The loud command bounced in echoes around the hall. Simmons thrust Rosalind from him as if she had infected him with the plague.

'She is wanton, sir,' he mumbled, 'leading me on. Any man would take what she just offered me.'

The officer's steel-grey eyes moved from Simmons to Rosalind, trying to accurately assess the situation before him.

'We have a difficult enough task, Simmons, and God knows we are hated enough already as it is in this area,' he said with impatience in his tone. 'Do you have to make it worse by assaulting every female in sight? In future, keep your lust for the tavern wenches. Now get out of here!'

Simmons picked up the sack without another word and left the hall.

Rosalind took a kerchief from her sleeve and wiped her mouth, intensely aware of the officer watching her. He moved towards her into the centre of the hall and a shaft of sunlight, streaming through a high window, rested on the sleek thickness of his black hair. His face was clean-shaven and unblemished, his lips fine, but at this moment set in a tight line. She met his gaze and saw not only hostility, but contempt in the steely gaze.

'I am Major Latimer,' he said in a voice as icy as his eyes. 'Be kind enough to inform your master that my men and I have arrived.'

She drew herself up, trying to maintain what little self-respect she had.

'I am Rosalind Pendrill, mistress of this manor. I do not have a master.'

He raised his eyebrows.

'Do you not? Well, I see a lady dressed in fine apparel, but your behaviour a minute since would have fooled anyone into believing you are a mere serving girl. I also recall it was you hanging out of a window for the benefit of my troopers. Do you usually make a habit of being friendly with soldiers?'

She gasped.

'You insult me, sir, to imagine I would demean myself in such a manner. That trooper assaulted me because I dared to question his right to steal my silver.'

'I would advise you to keep well away from my men whilst we are here, Mistress Pendrill. I am not satisfied the fault was all with trooper Simmons.'

Rosalind's anger rose at the disgust in his expression.

'Are you suggesting I may have encouraged him?'

'I did not observe you struggling to protect your virtue, quite the reverse. I believe you were enjoying his attentions!'

She was so infuriated by his derisory remarks, she raised her arm and without thought for the consequences slapped his face so hard he flinched. She stepped back, horrified. He gently fingered the red weal beginning to appear on his cheek and she knew if he retaliated she could blame no-one but herself. Done in the heat of anger, she now regretted her foolish action.

'Please forgive me, my behaviour is inexcusable,' she murmured, her cheeks burning with mortification.

'Think yourself fortunate you are a woman!'

His voice washed over her like waves of cold water.

'If you were a man, you would pay dearly for such action!'

He turned abruptly and began to walk away.

'Major Latimer!' she called.

He turned to face her, his features a taut mask. She took a step towards him, her anger matching his own.

'Remember one fact, sir. This was my home long before you and your band of rebels came here and how I act is my business. I do not recognise your authority, nor will I be ordered about like one of your men. I furthermore consider you are nothing but a traitor to your lawful king and the sooner your kind is strung from a gibbet the better!'

The hot tirade poured from her, but she was past caring. He moved closer and she had to tilt her head to look into his eyes.

'Have you finished, Mistress Pendrill?' His tone was softly menacing. 'You play a dangerous game. Do you want me to retaliate for this?'

He touched the red mark on his cheek.

'I have spoken the truth. If you deem

it worthy of retaliation, then do so,' she challenged.

His gaze moved over her face and hair and she saw, in the grey depths of his eyes, a hint of admiration.

'You are a brave woman, but you hold no importance. What is important is that this war is won by Parliament and we need all the funds we can obtain, including your silver.'

'So Parliament steals what it cannot gain by lawful means?' she taunted.

A frown creased his forehead.

'This conflict has not been instigated by Parliament, but by an intransigent monarch who has closed his ears to the cries of his subjects.'

'Surely a king is above his subjects,' she questioned. 'Charles Stuart is reigning by Divine Right. We cannot judge his actions.'

'He is a vain man, guilty of errors, as we all are, but he has raised himself above us mortal beings, believing he is answerable to no-one.'

'I am of a mind to think your greatest

error was choosing to support Parliament, Major Latimer.'

His features darkened and she shrank inwardly, realising her remark had antagonised him further.

'My errors are not your concern, Mistress Pendrill. You would be wise to speak and act with more decorum in the future. To get back to the matter of your silver, you will be reimbursed in due course, have no doubt of that.'

Rosalind sensed he was having difficulty keeping his anger in check and anxious to end the conversation, she made to move past him. A nervous, dizzy attack brought her swaying close to him and he reached out to steady her. His hands fastened around her waist and very slowly he drew her into the circle of his arms. She knew what was about to happen, but could not move as his head lowered and his lips touched her own.

It was insane but she didn't want the kiss to end. She pressed herself against his hard frame, feeling pleasure curl her stomach when his hands began to caress her. The moment was shattered for Rosalind when he suddenly released her.

'Perhaps my first assessment of you was correct after all, but it will not work with me, mistress. I am not as gullible to your feminine wiles as my troopers are.'

The scorn in his voice stung her to silence. He turned and strode to the outer door, disappearing into the sunlit courtyard. An icy chill swept over her body. What must he think of her reacting to his kiss so brazenly? He was another formidable force to be reckoned with and the prospect was very daunting at that moment!

3

Rosalind was summoned to the oak-panelled withdrawing-room. The tall windows gave panoramic views across the wide, sweeping lawns leading down to the lake, which cast shimmering waves of blue light in the dying rays of the evening sun. Nathaniel was surveying the scene when Rosalind entered. She waited until he turned to give her his attention.

'I wish to discuss a very important matter with you, Rosalind. Please be seated.'

He drew forward a high-backed chair for her and then seated himself behind the sturdy, oak desk, upon which were strewn various documents.

'I have been perusing briefly through some of the ledgers of the estate and quite frankly I am appalled at the disastrous situation the estate is in since

I last had access to the accounts. It seems certain your brother was more concerned in fighting for a lost cause then ensuring his livelihood and future were secure. He has certainly given no thought for you!'

'Most of the money has gone towards helping the King. Thomas provides as well as he can with what little there is left!' she answered sharply, furious Nathaniel had taken it upon himself to pry into their affairs.

'Yes, to the ruination of you both!' he snapped. 'You must realise these debts have mounted up to such a degree that very soon you will have creditors howling at your door and the manor will be the asking price. We must settle this matter as soon as possible.'

'You are no longer our family lawyer,' she said coldly. 'Please do not meddle where you are not welcome!'

'We both know there is a sure way of putting the estate back to rights and it is in your hands only. As you are aware, when you marry, your dowry will be released. I made out the document some years past so I know it is a very substantial amount.'

'Since I am not intending to marry in the near future, the dowry cannot be released,' she replied in clipped tones.

His indulgent manner evaporated.

'What about your loyal servants? Their livelihood depends on the good management of this household. Surely you do not want to have your servants sent away and your land sold off to pay the debts?'

'It will not come to anything as drastic as that!'

'I advise you to think very deeply on the matter. Marry me and all your problems will be solved. It is what your father wished for you.'

'My father would never have been agreeable to me marrying you! You cannot force me into this.'

'It is not a matter of force, but commonsense, Rosalind. You are alone, with no means of support. When the war is over there will be no restoration of Royalist property when Parliament is in control.'

'How can you be so certain Parliament will win. The king will not concede defeat so easily.'

Nathaniel eyed her with an expression he would give an innocent child.

'Because, my dear, we are gaining the upper hand in almost every campaign. The defeat for the Royalist forces at Marston Moor last year placed the whole of the north of England in our power. Another major confrontation will only seal Charles Stuart's doom.'

Rosalind moved to the window and stared out, unmindful of the peaceful scene. She knew what he said was true, but was unwilling to acknowledge it. She was startled when iron-hard fingers dug into her arms.

'Imagine what we can achieve for the good of the manor. It needs an heir, a new life blood to give back respect and dignity to the estate.'

She whirled to face him, her eyes blazing with fury.

'My brother, Thomas, is the present owner and it will be his offspring who will restore the fortunes of this house.'

He smiled indulgently.

'I have already warned you he is most likely dead.'

She brushed past him and walked quickly from the room. He appeared to relish the fact of Thomas's possible death. The dreadful thing was she was beginning to believe it might be true. She was gradually succumbing to Nathaniel's forceful influence and God help her if she lost the spirit to fight.

A short while later, Rosalind was descending the staircase to see that Nathaniel and the major were already seated at the table in the hall. Alerted by the soft rustle of her skirts, they rose to their feet. She earned a look of reproach from Nathaniel when she seated herself at the lower end of the table, well away from them. Major Latimer eyed her with a keen scrutiny.

Despite her prudent management of the household supplies, it appeared

Nathaniel had overruled her orders to the kitchen to supply plain fare. She eyed the abundant meal with silent anger, but not wishing to confront Nathaniel again that day, she ate sparingly of the delicious food.

Rosalind made a mental note to tell Mistress Larch, the cook, to use up the leftovers the following day.

During the meal, the two men discussed the way the war was going in their favour. Rosalind listened in silence, wondering at the quirk of fate which had brought her, after three long, brutal years of conflict, to be sitting at a table, sharing a meal with her enemies.

'I understand your father, Sir Henry, did not involve himself in the war, Mistress Pendrill. Is that true?'

Rosalind raised her head to find the major's steel gaze fixed on her.

'That is so, Major Latimer. What of it?'

'Surely at times like these, one cannot sit on the fence, so to speak,' he replied.

'My father was a landowner, not a soldier or politician,' she said tartly.

'No-one can remain neutral in a civil war, unless it furthers their own gains.'

His voice was heavy with sarcasm.

'My father was ill the last years of his life. He could not take up arms, but I can assure you he was loyal to his king!'

Rosalind's voice rose in vigorous defence of her father.

'Then if that was so, I am suitably chastised.'

The major's voice was edged with mockery. Nathaniel snorted in derision.

'I seem to bring to mind your father was not ill at the start of these troubles, yet he was not present at Edgehill.'

Rosalind's gaze rested on him with unconcealed revulsion.

'I do not believe I have heard of your exploits on the field of battle,' she parried verbally, knowing Nathaniel had stayed away from taking part personally in any conflict.

Nathaniel's features darkened as the barb hit home. Glancing at the major,

Rosalind noted his lips were curved in the ghost of a smile and she felt a surge of satisfaction.

'Beware your ambitions are not your noose, sir!' she returned.

'My lady here has been dabbling in dangerous games, Francis. I have warned her that giving aid to fugitive malignants could be at a high price.'

Nathaniel's eyes were deep pools of blackness as he fixed his gaze with malice on her whitening features. A cold hand circled Rosalind's heart. He had promised not to inform the authorities, but now the major knew, would he take the matter further?

A thoughtful expression narrowed Francis' eyes as he studied Rosalind.

'Dangerous games indeed,' he murmured, 'but I think you have already paid a high price in the sequestration of your home.'

'Yes, sir, it is surely a high price for helping my friends. I merely gave accommodation to those who needed it.'

'It is a different matter when those you accommodate are close to the King and carry important dispatches!' Nathaniel cut in.

'You have no proof the man you sought was here. He would deem it unwise to entrust himself with important King's business in a house surrounded by rebel forces!' she scoffed, trying to hide her fear.

'We are both well aware John Verney did just that!'

'By what I have heard, I perceive you have escaped lightly, Miss Pendrill, if sequestration is your only punishment!' Francis Latimer said, his piercing steel gaze threatening to cut through her composure. 'At least there will be a halt to your dubious activities!'

The warning in the major's tone was clear and a shudder ran through her. She feared Nathaniel, but Latimer, she realised, was a man with the ruthless streak of a soldier, backed by a disciplined military force — a man who would deal severely with his enemies!

She swallowed hard on the lump in her throat. Self-pity and grief rose at odd times and she wanted to sob bitterly because she was alone without her father and brother there to defend her, but she could not weep before her enemies so she sat there, stone faced. How could he say her punishment was light? Everything had just been taken away from her and she was left with nothing!

Rosalind was awoken early next morning by the troopers gathering in the courtyard. She left her bed to go to the window and gaze on the activity outside. They did not intend to waste Parliament's time, she thought ruefully. She was about to return to bed, when the major strode into the courtyard with Nathaniel at his side.

It was clear he and his troopers meant business in their routing of Royalist factions, but despite her hatred she found she could not take her eyes from him. He had not yet donned his helmet and the sun shone on the sleek waves of his shoulder-length hair. She began to wish he was not on the wrong side in the war. If things were different and he supported the King, she would now be viewing him as a friend and ally.

She returned to bed and the remembrance of his lips drawing an undeniable response from her rose again in her mind. She suddenly realised the way her thoughts were taking her and she cringed with self loathing. He was an enemy and loathing was all she should feel, yet deep within herself she was aware that among her feelings of fear and loathing was a spark of interest in the Roundhead major that had nothing to do with the war!

Rosalind sought out William, her steward, after she had breakfasted. He informed her the troopers had indeed gone on patrol to find pockets of Royalist resistance. Nathaniel had ridden to Chichester on a personal matter, and he could stay there, she thought mutinously.

The soldiers left on guard seemed

very lax and spent much of their time in the kitchen, drinking ale, much to Mistress Larch's disapproval. This gave Rosalind the freedom of much of the house.

It was a lovely, warm day and the gardens were a riot of May flowers. She turned to face the sun as she strolled leisurely through the rose garden, towards the fountain and leaned over the deep, wide perimeter, thinking of the night she and John Verney had scrambled over the rim, to run quickly to the orchard and safety. Would she ever know if his mission to reach the King's secretary had been accomplished?

It was here, long ago, she and Thomas used to play in the sparkling water that gushed from the iron gargoyles high at the top of the stonework. They had always been close as brother and sister and sadness filled her that those innocent childhood days were gone for ever. Was Thomas really dead? A sense within her told her not to give up hope.

She straightened and out of the corner of her eye she saw a movement near the gateway to the orchard. She strained her eyesight to cover the distance and saw a man lurking furtively, almost as if he didn't want to be seen, then she realised he was beckoning to her. With a rush of joy she realised it was Thomas! She began to walk slowly along the path, trying not to hurry and bring attention to herself. The way seemed endless, but at last in the shelter of the trees, she was reunited with the brother she had come close to believing was dead!

'I thought I would never see you again, Tom!' she said, hugging him close. 'Nathaniel Black said there were reports you'd been killed in a skirmish at Siddlesham.'

'The lying toad! I have not been near Siddlesham. Why should he spread false rumours concerning my welfare?'

'He has sequestered the manor, Tom, in Parliament's name. I think he desires your death so he can have our home for himself!'

Thomas's lips drew into a tight line.

'The minute my back is turned the vulture strikes! I left my horse at Ned Holden's and he informed me the Roundheads were here, but he mentioned nothing about Nathaniel Black. He did say you have been hiding Royalists.'

A frown knitted his brows together.

'You must not do so again, Ros. It's too dangerous. If they had caught you, I dread to think . . . '

His voice trailed off as she put a finger to his lips.

'There is no need for concern, Tom. My part in helping the cause is over, I fear. There is no possibility of bringing anyone here with all these soldiers billeted around the grounds.'

Thomas leaned wearily against a tree trunk.

'You look in need of rest, Tom. We can't stay here. Someone may see you. Nathaniel is away in Chichester today and most of the troopers are out patrolling the area.'

'I dare not stay, Ros. I came only to see you.'

He straightened and she clung to his arm, afraid he would leave.

'Why not hide in the secret room for a few hours?' she suggested. 'I need to talk to you. If we are careful, the troopers left on guard will not see you. They spend most of their time in the kitchen anyway.'

'I mustn't place you in any danger,' he replied, undecided.

There were lines of strain around his mouth and she realised he was no longer the carefree Cavalier in fine clothes of lace and feathers. In his buff jerkin and serge breeches he could be taken for one of Parliament's men. It was in his expression where she noted the greatest change. He looked sombre with a world weariness she had not seen in him before. The war had taken its toll on her brother and she felt a surge of anger at the perpetrators who had started the heinous conflict.

'Danger is second nature to me since the Roundheads arrived,' she said, in a light-hearted attempt to conceal from him just how precarious her position was. 'Follow me, but stay well behind until we reach the house.'

All was quiet when Rosalind entered the stone-flagged passage and she turned to beckon Thomas to follow. He joined her, then suddenly the door at the end of the passage opened and they both exhaled their breath when they saw it was only Mary. Her face lit up at the sight of her master.

'Are there any troopers on the upper floor, Mary?' Rosalind whispered.

'No, mistress, they've just gone to the kitchen. I'll go and keep 'em occupied.'

'Bless you, Mary. Thomas is going to stay here for a few hours until he has rested sufficiently.'

Mary went back to the kitchen, while Rosalind and Thomas hurried up the rear staircase. When they reached the bedchamber where the secret room was situated, she moved to the fireplace and pressed on part of the panelling to one side of the mantelpiece. The panel swung outwards, revealing a dark aperture. Rosalind stepped into the darkness, holding high the candle she had just lit.

She waited for Thomas to join her then pressed a lever which closed the panel from the inside. The small, claustrophobic room contained only a truckle bed and a table and chair. The manor had been built by a Catholic family and they had made the secret room to hide priests, when the Protestant faith was seeking to establish itself.

She felt intense anger at being reduced to creeping around their own home like felons. Some of her frustration went into the effort of pulling off her brother's leather, bucket-top boots. Thomas smiled, unaware her thoughts were directed in anger at the Roundheads. There was so much she wanted to ask him, but she realised it would have to wait until he had rested. She left him to sleep, promising to return later with food and ale.

As she pressed the panel back into place, she glanced around the room, realising with a start this was the chamber Francis Latimer had been given. There was evidence of his occupancy in the fine lawn shirt flung carelessly across the bed and one or two other items, a brush, shaving implements and a black velvet doublet draped over a chair. She crossed the room and ran her hand over the silky fabric. She bent her head to catch a faint tang of soap and an indefinable scent which belonged to him alone. Rosalind pulled herself up sharp. What was she doing? There were more important matters than mooning over someone who was effectively her enemy.

She saved half her midday meal of bread, bacon and fruit and wrapped it in a cloth secreted under her skirts. It was more difficult with the ale, but she managed to hide a tankard under a shawl she carried over her arm. Thomas was awake and ready for something to eat. She was anxious to hear his news, but she waited patiently until he had finished eating.

'Tell me what has been happening, Tom. Did you meet Prince Rupert? Is he still holding Bristol? Are things really going badly for His Majesty?'

Thomas smiled at the torrent of questions pouring forth.

'It is true the war is not going too well for the cause. Even so, when I met the prince he appeared confident we can eventually triumph and bring these traitors to justice. My main task has been to recruit new men for the Royalist army, without much success, I'm afraid. Our supplies are short and conditions are appalling. Many who joined the King's army in the beginning are now deciding the rewards are not enough and are defecting to Parliament's side. Since Cromwell took over, the New Model army is receiving regular pay which we cannot promise.'

He stopped speaking and reached out his hand to brush a stray strand of hair from her face.

'Here I am, thinking only of myself. You must have been terrified when those rebels burst in. I should never have left the manor unguarded. What am I going to do with you?'

'Take me with you when you leave here!'

Her quick response to his question held a note of desperation.

'That is impossible. There is too much danger on the roads these days.'

'I'm not afraid and will face anything rather than remain here while Nathaniel thinks he is master. The way he looks at me chills me.'

Thomas was well aware the Puritan had more than a fatherly interest in his sister. In the past, he'd noticed Nathaniel watching Rosalind with blatant desire in his gaze. He silently swore that if Nathaniel ever attempted to touch his sister, he would deal very swiftly with him. Seeing the fear now in Rosalind's eyes when she spoke of him made him realise it would not be wise for her to remain at the manor without his protection.

'Very well, Ros, but it will not be an easy journey.'

'Where will we go?' she asked, but not really caring where as long as she was with Thomas.

'I have a friend and his wife in Bristol who will give you shelter. The town is held by us and you will be safe there during the times I will be about the King's business.'

'We must leave as soon as possible, Tom. The troopers may return at any moment and then it will be almost impossible to get away unseen.'

'Yes, you are right. We cannot wait for the cover of darkness. Go now quickly and collect what you need for the journey and meet me near the back door.'

'I wonder if we will ever return,' she whispered.

Thomas took her hands in his.

'Not if, but when, Ros. We will have our revenge on all these traitors and the first one to taste it will be Nathaniel Black!'

A shiver ran the length of her body and unbidden, Francis Latimer's face rose in her mind. The thought of him being at the end of Thomas's vengeance was very disturbing for a reason she could not understand.

She was collecting together the small items needed for the journey when the sudden return of the troopers in the courtyard below filled her with panic. She snatched up her small bag and, taking one last look around the room she had slept in all her life, she crept out on to the landing. The main door in the hall crashed back on its hinges and the shouts and laughter of the men entering the house made Rosalind flatten herself against the wall.

She began to move slowly, praying they would not notice her small, dark figure in the black cloak moving above them along the gallery. She passed the danger point and ran down the rear stairs. She was making her way to the door which opened on to the herb garden, when the door at the other end of the passage opened suddenly. It was too late to try and hide! The man who emerged from the kitchen had seen her!

'Well, if it ain't mistress high-and-mighty!'

Trooper Simmons' bulky frame filled the narrow passage. His gaze dropped to the bag she held and a sly smile widened his mouth.

'Not intending to leave us, are yer? That would be a pity when I have some unfinished business with yer to settle first.'

The outer door was just behind her, but to run would be futile. She would not take two steps before he would catch and overpower her.

'It is no concern of yours where I intend going,' she replied haughtily.

He moved quickly towards her and caught her arm in a tight grip.

'I fancy Major Latimer will be interested in your intentions, high-and-mighty mistress. Your journey will have to be postponed, I'm afraid.'

'Not this journey, Roundhead!' a voice hissed in a low whisper.

Simmons had no time to turn before he was felled to the floor by a heavy blow to his head. Rosalind hurried to Thomas.

'Is he dead?' she asked fearfully.

'No, I don't think so. The blow wasn't hard enough. He should be senseless long enough for us to get away!'

Thomas grabbed her hand and flung the candlestick he had used on Simmons to the floor. Neither of them spoke as they fled through the grounds, both realising what a narrow escape they'd had.

'Ned hasn't a spare horse,' Thomas said at last as they neared the blacksmith's. 'We'll have to share Spartan.'

When they arrived at Ned's cottage

he saddled Spartan and wished them God speed and a hope they could one day return to their home.

Rosalind hung on tightly behind Thomas when they finally set off. Whatever dangers they might face it could not rid her of the wonderful sense of freedom she now felt.

After several hours, Thomas suggested they stop for a rest at an inn he knew of not far away.

'The landlord is in sympathy with our cause and Spartan needs rest.'

Some while later, they entered the cobbled yard of the Red Fox. A stable lad heard their arrival and sauntered out to take charge of Spartan.

'Are there any military patrols in the inn, lad?' Thomas asked the boy.

'If yer mean Roundheads, sir, none here at present, but this area is swarming with 'em!'

Thomas frowned, wondering if it was such a good idea to stay after all. They entered the narrow passage and were welcomed by the landlord's wife who showed them into a parlour apart from the main tap-room. In a short time she had served them with large bowls of hot stew and fresh, crusty bread. The fire was warm and comforting and Rosalind began to feel drowsy. The hour was nearing midnight and she would have liked nothing better than to have stayed the night in a warm bed. Thomas arranged for her to have the use of a room for an hour to wash and freshen up.

She was shown to a tiny room at the rear of the inn and the landlord's wife brought a large jug and basin for her use. After washing her hands and face, she tried to tidy her hair as much as possible, but the wind had untangled the knot at the back of her head and it hung loose around her shoulders. It was hopeless to try and cope with it herself, so she gave up.

Rain began lashing against the window pane, making her glad they had stopped at the inn and were not riding out in the dark, hostile countryside. The bed was soft and inviting and she curled up on top of the thick covers and felt herself drifting into sleep. It was not for long, however, before there was a furious pounding on her door.

'Ros, open the door, quickly!' Thomas called.

She hurried to the door, her heart racing at the alarm in his voice.

'Roundheads just arrived! We must leave at once!'

He gave her time only to snatch up her cloak.

'My bag!' she cried, turning to go back.

'Leave it! I have to return later for Spartan, when I've found somewhere safe for you to wait.'

'No, Tom, you mustn't return here!'

He ignored her plea as they hurried down the stairs and along the passage.

'Hey, you two. Come here!' a loud, course voice hailed them.

Rosalind froze at the sound. It was trooper Simmons! Major Latimer had sent out men to search for her!

Simmons must not recognise her!

'Identify yourselves!' Simmons ordered, then his features altered into recognition. 'I know you, little mistress high-and-mighty. Hold fast there! Major Latimer wants to speak to you!'

Thomas had no intention of obeying the Roundhead. He caught Rosalind's hand and pulled her along the passage to the outer door. As they left the inn, Rosalind could hear Simmons shouting to the other troopers in the tap-room. Panic filled her to think the whole troop would shortly be pursuing them.

'There is a wood quite near here,' Thomas said. 'It's the only place in this area to hide. Can you run fast?'

'I'll do my best, Tom,' she cried against the strong wind and rain. 'That was the trooper you dealt the blow to. He must have recovered quickly.'

'More's the pity I did not hit him harder,' Tom muttered.

They reached the edge of a coppice and scrambled through the undergrowth.

'Leave me, Tom. You can escape. It doesn't matter about me!'

She had hardly got the words out when the silence was shattered by the loud explosion from a musket!

4

For a brief second the musket fire froze them to the spot, then Thomas caught Rosalind's arm.

'I'm not going without you, Ros,' he said with determination in his tone.

Pushing herself on with his firm hold on her arm, Rosalind had no idea how she managed to keep running. The rain was easing as they reached the shelter of the wood. The clouds were parting, allowing silvers of moonlight to slant through the trees, relieving the pitch blackness. The shouts of the troopers pursuing them eventually receded into the distance.

After what seemed an eternity the trees began to thin out and they emerged out of the wood on to a dirt track. Within a few minutes of walking, the dark outline of a cottage appeared. They walked around to the rear and found a ramshackle barn. Thomas pushed open the door and peered in.

'This appears a good place to wait, Ros.'

In a corner were bales of straw and he took off his cloak and placed it over the bales, making a bed of sorts for her.

'Rest here,' he said, waiting until she had settled herself on the straw before walking to the door. 'I must keep watch in case the Roundheads are still pursuing us. If all remains quiet I will go back to the inn for Spartan.'

Rosalind jumped up in alarm.

'No! You must promise me you will go nowhere near that inn yet!'

'We will get nowhere without Spartan!' he answered impatiently.

'Wait until the danger is past,' she urged. 'The Roundheads may move on eventually, then we can return to the inn.'

Several emotions crossed his features.

'Very well,' he relented. 'We will wait here until dawn.'

She settled back on the straw and

huddled into her damp cloak, shivering uncontrollably for a long time, but eventually she drifted off to sleep. She was icy cold when she awoke. She sat up, glancing around in the grey dawn light for Thomas. He was standing near the door, looking out. At the sound of her awakening, he smiled.

'Did you sleep well?' he asked, stifling a yawn.

'Yes, thank you. I can see it is almost daylight. Why didn't you wake me? I could have taken my turn in keeping watch.'

'Don't worry about me, I'm fine. We must be on our way now. I have to try and get Spartan before the Roundheads are up and about.'

The sky was beginning to lighten with the new day as they walked back along the track towards the woods. High above them in the branches of the trees, the birds were in full song with their dawn chorus. When the Red Fox came into view, Thomas halted.

'Wait here for me, Ros. Stay out of

sight of the road until I return.'

He was about to walk on, but she clutched his sleeve, a sense of foreboding niggling at her.

'The troopers may be on watch for you. Leave Spartan. The landlord will take care of him. We can buy another horse.'

'Leave Spartan, to be sold? No, that horse means too much to me. I will not give him up!'

'Will you risk your freedom for the sake of a horse?' she asked in exasperation at his stubbornness.

He ignored her remark.

'I won't be long.'

He bent to kiss her cheek and she clung to him for a precious minute, feeling very afraid for him. She hid among some bushes and watched until he crept out of sight into the inn yard. The waiting was agonising. She was in such a high state of nervous tension, eventually she could wait no longer. Something must have gone wrong. If Thomas had been captured, then the

Roundheads could have her as well! She had no intention of carrying on with her journey without him. Where could she go? She did not know where in Bristol his friends were.

The inn lay slumbering in the first grey light of the day, not yet awakened by its occupants as she entered the yard and walked cautiously towards the table. All was silent. Where on earth was Thomas? She dare not call him for fear someone heard her. She slowly pushed open the heavy stable door. The sight which greeted her froze her to the spot, then sent her hurrying to where Thomas lay, bound hand and foot with a gag across his mouth. She was uncaring of the danger to herself or that the whole scene was a trap.

She kneeled down beside him and untied the gag. Thomas barely had time to croak a warning before strong hands gripped her arms and pulled her to her feet. She spun round and came face to face with Francis Latimer!

'If you had designs on rescuing your

friend, you should have made your plans more carefully, Mistress Pendrill.'

His expression held a glint of triumph in his steel gaze, and with a deep sigh her shoulders slumped in resignation.

'What are you intending to do with us?' she asked in a dispirited voice.

'Return you to your home,' he replied curtly. 'The fate of your companion is another matter. He has the death of one of my troopers to account for.'

Her gaze followed his and she saw the body of a trooper laid lifeless in a corner of the stable. She turned shocked eyes to Thomas and wanted to shout and rail at him for being so foolish in returning to the inn and not heeding her warning.

'Why should he have to account for his actions? This is a time of war! To who do you account for your sins, Major Latimer?' she taunted.

He stared at her, his mouth fixed in a tight line.

'At this precise moment, no-one, but

you do, to Master Black. I hope you can give a justified account of why you were fleeing with your lover!'

'Lover! You think Thomas and I are lovers?'

She could barely suppress the laughter which bubbled up.

'Thomas is my brother!'

The harshness in Francis' expression relaxed as her words sunk in.

'Your brother? Forgive me, I did not know. I can understand your brother's motives in seeking to protect you, but it still does not excuse his actions. For the death of my trooper, hc will be taken to Chichester for trial.'

Rosalind gave him a look of pure contempt.

'You do your duty exceedingly well, Major Latimer. Perhaps for this day's work you will be in line for promotion.'

'Sarcasm will not help your brother, Mistress Pendrill. He was very foolish returning here, but it has saved me the job of scouring the countryside for you. I will arrange with the inn-keeper to provide you with a private room where you can take your meal and rest.'

'Please do not bother on my behalf, Major Latimer. I will not eat until I am assured Thomas will be treated with decency.'

'I am not intending to starve him!' he answered curtly.

'Perhaps not, but you intend that he should be executed!' she retorted.

'It is my task to carry out orders, mistress. Nathaniel returned to the manor shortly after you fled and was concerned for your safety.'

'He is concerned for nothing and no-one but his ambitions!' she replied with an acid tone. 'Tell me, how did you know the direction we travelled?'

'Simmons recovered swiftly and we set out immediately. A pedlar we stopped remembered seeing a man and woman sharing a horse. It took very little to fathom it was you and your brother.'

'You are nothing but a lackey for that Puritan, jumping to do his bidding so promptly,' she answered with contempt.

His expression darkened and he took a step towards her. She turned and walked quickly across the yard and entered the inn, but she had not gone far along the dim, narrow passage when he caught up with her and, grasping her arm, twisted her round to face him.

'I am no-one's lackey! You need to curb your tongue. There are many who are not as tolerant as I am and would seek retribution for your ill-thought words!'

His voice was low and well-controlled, but there was a tenseness in his body which belied his words.

'If you do not like what I say that is your concern!' she taunted.

'You say too much for your own good, Mistress Pendrill. My task is to return you to your home and your brother to gaol where he belongs.'

'Please allow Thomas to go free,' she pleaded. 'His motives were purely to help me and he must have killed that trooper out of necessity.'

'He has committed a crime. If I was lenient with every stray malignant I captured, parliament would never see an end to this war.'

His voice was harsh and uncompromising.

'I will do anything you ask, if you will release my brother,' she pleaded again, grasping at his sleeve.

He glanced down at the taut, white knuckles of her small hand. A faint smile curved his lips.

'Am I actually hearing a Royalist begging a favour from a Roundhead? I wonder just what you would be willing to do? Perhaps this?'

He pressed her forcefully back against the wall and bent his head. His expression gave her a warning, but it was too late to escape the pressure of his mouth meeting her own. All that mattered was that Thomas should gain his freedom. If Francis Latimer wanted her as his bargaining point, then he could have her. As his kiss deepened the remembrance of his first kiss came into her chaotic thoughts.

She had been stunned then by her reaction to his kiss, but now her whole body was tingling with desire for him. Jonathan, her betrothed, who had died at the Battle of Edgehill, had never set her on fire as this man was doing. Her arms reached around his neck and caught in the thick waves of his hair.

The war, their animosity, the fact he was a traitor meant nothing. She had never felt this way about any man, yet she knew she should fight the attraction she felt for him. It could only end in pain and heartbreak for her. He was her enemy and could never be anything else while the war lasted.

He suddenly released her and stood back.

'I must be going insane, but I won't apologise as I believe you gained as much enjoyment as I did. I think it wise if we both forget it happened.'

'As I am insane for allowing you to touch me,' she said, putting a trembling hand to her mouth.

He turned abruptly and walked down the passage without a backward glance. Rosalind fingered her lips, bruised by the hard passion of his kiss. Nathaniel had warned her Francis possessed a ruthless streak when he was resolved on a matter, a ruthlessness far more dangerous to her peace of mind than Nathaniel possessed.

The landlord gave Rosalind the chamber she had occupied earlier. She had brought a small mirror with her and she stared into it while she attempted to brush out the tangles in her hair. The forceful strokes were a combination of frustration at Thomas's captivity, of being caught so easily and the fact that her own body could betray her with one embrace. Even now her lips tingled with the memory of that forceful kiss. He had taken her unawares and she was ashamed it was having such an impact on her. She could not forget it even though he had said it was better they both put it from their minds.

The day passed slowly. For half of the time, Rosalind slept in the soft bed. Then it was evening and there was no sign the intended journey to Pendrill Manor would be accomplished that day. Her frustration increased as the sound of laughter downstairs drifted up to her. The troopers must be well inebriated by now and probably had no intention of leaving.

There was a light tap on her door and when she opened it her heart began to beat quicker at the sight of Francis. She searched his features for some sign their earlier passionate encounter had affected him, but seeing his cold, remote expression it seemed the event that had turned the world upside down was forgotten in his mind.

'Mistress Pendrill, you may be glad to know I have decided to remain here until the morning. It is more sensible to commence our journey in daylight and the men need time to relax. As we are leaving at eight, I suggest you retire early in readiness for the journey.'

'It appears I have no choice. My life is not my own anymore.'

His lips were compressed in an unyielding line and she thought of the time when she had felt those lips, warm and demanding, drawing the very soul from her body. How could he act as if it had never happened?'

'Are any of us in control of our own lives?' he remarked, equally bitter.

Without another word he swung round and strode away down the dark landing. Rosalind closed her door and leaned back against it. She meant nothing to him, but a responsibility to be relieved of when they reached the manor. She went to bed feeling utterly miserable.

The commotion in the yard below brought Rosalind fully awake in a second. She sprang out of bed and ran to the window. The stable was to one side of the inn and from her room she could see very little when she opened the casement and leaned out. She could hear a scuffle in the yard below and someone shouting as the troopers filed out of the inn. She began to feel afraid for Thomas. Had he been harmed? She must find out!

Closing the window, she moved to the bed, where she had left her gown draped. There was no time to put it on before her door crashed back on its hinges. Francis entered, kicking the door closed behind him with his foot. His features were set into a taut mask of fury.

'Do you make a habit of thrusting yourself uninvited into a lady's bed-chamber?' she asked coldly.

'If you had taken the precaution of locking your door then I would have been unable to!'

He could barely suppress his rage as his icy gaze slid the length of her partially-clad figure.

'What a pity they could not include you in their little plan. It was not gallant leaving you to our mercy,' he fumed.

'I don't know what you are talking about. What has happened?' she asked, mystified, then she gasped in fear as his control snapped and he narrowed the gap between them and gripped her arms.

'Don't play the innocent with me!' he stormed. 'All the time you were pleading with me to free your brother, you had this little plot all worked out. You certainly fooled me with your soft lips and yielding body.'

'Has Thomas escaped?'

Relief bubbled up in her.

'I know of no plan to free him. No-one knew we were here, but whoever has freed him should be saluted for their bravery.'

'Yes, salute them,' he sneered. 'They were so brave they stabbed two of my men in the back. Now tell me all Royalists fight like gentlemen!'

He released her and began to pace up and down, a pensive look on his dark features. He halted and once again his steel grey eyes slid over her. His mouth curled in cynicism when she crossed her arms over her chest.

'It will serve no purpose now to pursue your brother. I have lost too many men since yesterday. I came solely to search for you. I am certain there will be other opportunities to capture him. He is sure to try and contact you sooner or later and when he does I will be waiting for him!'

His keen scrutiny scanned her face, missing nothing of the sadness in her dark eyes.

'Are you not happy your brother is free?'

'I would have been far happier if I was with him now. All I have to look forward to is returning to a place I can no longer call home. I am afraid of what Nathaniel may do when I return to the manor.'

Francis moved to the door.

'Believe me, Mistress Pendrill, he will not harm you or he will answer to me. There is nothing to fear by returning to your home.'

With that surprising statement he left the room.

Rosalind returned to bed, mulling over what Francis had said. He had in fact made a promise that he would protect her against Nathaniel's anger. A tremor ran through her to think that it was somehow a link between her and Francis. At best it was a tenuous link, but one she strangely welcomed.

Next morning, Rosalind was breakfasting alone, when the innkeeper came into the parlour and seated himself beside her. He seemed ill at ease and glanced continually towards the door.

'I'll be brief, mistress. You never know who might be listening at doors these days,' he said in hushed whispers. 'Two friends of mine were visiting here last evening and I happened to mention how you and your brother were hoping to reach Bristol, but were side-tracked, so to speak, by the Roundheads. My friends thought it a shame your brother be on the way to gaol when the King's army needs him so badly. They were sorry they could not include you in their plans for escape.'

'I care not for myself, Master Smith. I cannot thank your friends enough for freeing my brother. If it were not for your intervention I do not know what fate Thomas would have faced,' she whispered.

'Worry no longer, mistress. Your brother has been taken to a safe house, some thirty miles from here.'

The sound of someone outside the door brought Giles Smith swiftly to his feet. He bade her a safe journey before leaving the room. She walked to the window and saw the three dead men being hoisted over the saddles of their horses. Francis emerged from the stable, leading his horse. Her gaze moved over the waving abundance of his dark hair and her breath caught on a deep sigh. Why couldn't the wretched war end? Things might have been so different between them if the barrier of Royalist and Parliamentarian did not exist.

5

On her return to the manor, Rosalind waited with bated breath for Nathaniel's anger to descend, but as time went on he continued to treat her with cool courtesy. She wondered if Francis had somehow persuaded Nathaniel to restrain his anger. Her main concern now was to try and overcome the bitter disappointment of having her hopes dashed of a new life in Bristol. Her only consolation was the fact of Thomas's freedom.

One morning, Nathaniel informed her he was riding to Chichester regarding legal matters. While he was absent, she took the opportunity to search the desk in the drawing-room. All the estate documents, she discovered, had been removed. She slammed the desk drawers shut in frustrated anger. What had he done with them, she wondered. Had he gone to Chichester to legalise the sequestration of the manor?

A shiver of unease ran through her. Where did that leave Thomas as legal heir? She moved to the fireplace and gazed up at the portrait of her father, Sir Henry Pendrill. Thank goodness, she thought, he had not lived to endure the humiliation she and Thomas were now experiencing. Could he ever have envisaged such a deplorable situation, a mere lawyer making himself master of someone's property, with Parliament's approval!

'Rest assured, Father,' she muttered in a fierce tone, 'I will never yield to any traitor while I have breath in my body, least of all to Nathaniel Black!'

'Strong sentiments, Mistress Pendrill. I hope you can live up to them!'

She spun round, startled by the deep, masculine voice. Francis was leaning in a relaxed manner against the door frame. She wondered how long he had been watching her.

'You startled me, Major Latimer!' she exclaimed, feeling a rush of colour in her cheeks at his sudden appearance.

He was wearing the black velvet doublet she had seen in his room and her heart raced at how much younger and darkly handsome he appeared without the trappings of warfare. He walked into the room and joined her by the fireplace.

'Surely we can dispense with formalities, Rosalind. Major Latimer sounds so formal and I think we are well enough acquainted to use our first names. Please call me Francis.'

Her heart somersaulted at his suggestion they regard one another on more intimate terms.

'You appeared to be very agitated just now. Has Nathaniel been issuing his orders again?' he asked.

'No, it isn't that. I was reflecting on what my father's reaction would have been to know his house and lands are confiscated by Parliament, especially knowing the man who professed to be

92

my family's loyal friend has usurped Thomas's place as the manor's heir.'

'I am sorry I can do nothing to help you in this matter, Rosalind. One day, when this wretched war is over, I am sure sequestered property will be restored to the rightful owners.'

'How can any of us be certain of what will happen in the future? I dread to contemplate what the outcome will be.'

'This madness has to end sometime, for all our sakes,' he answered vehemently. 'We must all strive for peace and justice.'

'I wonder if we will ever see those again in England.'

'It will happen sooner or later and I for one long for the war to end. So many lives have been shattered. My brother was killed at the Battle of Edgehill, then I watched my own father killed on the battlefield at Marston Moor before my very eyes. He was a Royalist, but I would have saved him if it had been possible. Now there is only my mother left.'

The pain of his loss was clearly revealed in his eyes and Rosalind realised this was a side of Francis Latimer she had not seen before. Grief rose within her for him and at the memory of her father's death three months before and the loss of her betrothed, Jonathan.

'Do you not have a family of your own?'

'If you mean a wife and children, no I haven't, yet.'

His lips curved in a wry smile at the delicate shade of pink on her cheeks.

'I can understand your grief,' she replied. 'I lost my betrothed at Edgehill. We were to have been wed on his return. Then I lost my father of natural causes recently.'

'I am sorry to hear of your bereavements. It must have been very distressing to lose your betrothed in that violent way.'

His keen gaze took in the shadows which crossed her face.

'Yes, it was, but that was three years ago and time dulls the pain.'

'You are intelligent and beautiful, Rosalind. I cannot believe you have no other suitors.'

His appreciative gaze swept over her face and hair.

'Nathaniel wishes to marry me.'

Francis's expression darkened with anger.

'That man thinks to court you? He is not worthy to touch a hair of your head! Surely you will not consider such a union.'

'I am alone with little means of support. Nathaniel is a wealthy man in his own right. As I no longer own my home, it seems sensible to marry him.'

She tried to convince herself as she was speaking that there really were advantages in becoming Nathaniel's wife.

'You must not marry him. I have seen the loathing in your eyes when you look at him. Don't throw your life away!'

There was real anger in his tone.

'What is it to you? The estate is in dire trouble. Nathaniel will pay off the debts with my dowry. I will do anything to save the manor.'

She kept her eyes averted from his intense gaze.

'So bricks and mortar mean more to you than your own happiness,' he jeered. 'All this will be here when you are long gone. How will I feel when you have to bed with Nathaniel?'

She backed away from him, the horror showing clearly in her eyes.

'How dare you talk to me like this! It is not your concern whom I marry!'

His lips lifted in wry amusement.

'Oh, but I think it is. When a woman kisses me as you did, I do not believe she is ready to marry another man. Think about it, Rosalind.'

She was left in stunned silence as he drew away and left the room.

Later, in bed, mulling over Francis's last remark she knew he spoke truthfully. When he held her in his arms, nothing else mattered. She had seen a gentler side of him that day and if he had offered marriage she would gladly have accepted. The reason why was one she had been reluctant to admit to herself since Francis had kissed her at the inn. She loved him! How it had happened when he represented all she detested she did not know, but the love that had come to her could be denied no longer. An insidious little voice crept into her head.

What are you think of? He is one of the enemy and you are betraying all you profess to believe in! Was it betrayal of the cause to love one of the enemy? The doubts swam round in her head until she could have wept. She must accept that Francis would never return her love. She spent a very disturbed night and only fell into a fitful sleep when dawn appeared.

The following day, Nathaniel was in the parlour, scrutinising a document which had just arrived. Francis was leaning against the mantelpiece, watching him with a sombre expression.

'Let us hope this may be the final battle which will seal the fate of Charles Stuart, once and for all, Francis.'

Nathaniel tapped the document with exuberance.

'I sincerely hope so,' Francis agreed thoughtfully. 'The King does not possess the fighting force now to match ours.'

At that moment, Rosalind entered the parlour. Alerted by her entry, they both turned. She was wearing a gown in a deep shade of emerald satin and she felt a glow of pleasure when she saw admiration in Francis's gaze.

'My dear, important news has arrived.'

Nathaniel drew her towards the high-backed settle near the hearth.

'Major Latimer has been recalled to London to receive orders. It appears there may be an imminent battle and all available troops are being mobilised.'

Rosalind stared at Francis, but his set features revealed nothing of the possible turmoil he was in.

'When are you leaving?' she asked in a small, cold voice.

'We are preparing to leave almost immediately the evening meal is over,' he replied, his voice betraying no emotion.

During the meal, she could barely swallow the food set before her and as soon as she was able, she excused herself and went immediately to her room. She paced restlessly up and down, cursing herself for the longing which was tearing her apart — the longing for Francis to take her in his arms one last time. He was going to battle again and might never return! She had to see him before he left the manor! She smoothed a trembling hand over her hair and walked on to the landing. As if her prayer had been answered, she encountered Francis coming towards her.

'Are you leaving now?' she asked, trying to sound disinterested, but not succeeding.

'No doubt you welcome my departure, but why do I see only misery and no relief in your eyes?'

She cursed herself for being unable to conceal her feelings.

'I do not find it pleasurable to hear there may be another major battle. Remember, I have a brother who may be involved.'

'I have not forgotten, and one day Thomas Pendrill will be brought to account,' he stated in a chilling tone.

A thread of fear coursed through her. She could not forget the fact he was still intent on bringing Thomas to justice for his killing of the trooper at the inn.

'It is possible we may never see one another again,' he said in a low voice, moving so close to her she felt the whisper of his breath on her cheek. 'Promise me you will not marry Nathaniel.'

'I cannot promise, Francis. Events may force me to it, even though I loathe the very thought!'

'As indeed I loathe the very thought of that Puritan touching as much as a hair on your head!'

He reached out and caught one of her ringlets. She shivered as his fingers caressed her neck.

'You should not say such things to me. We are enemies and can ever be anything more!'

She met his gaze, unwavering.

'Never is a long time, Rosalind. One day this war will be over. Will I still be your enemy then?'

Rosalind drew a deep breath.

'You will not be my enemy now if you promise not to pursue my brother, if you survive the battle, that is.'

'Ah, yes, that little word if.'

He stared at her, deep in thought.

'I cannot make that promise. I am commissioned to bring about Parliament's aims. If your brother involves himself in trying to destroy those aims, then I must ensure he faces the consequences.'

Rosalind recoiled from him.

'Then I make no promise that I will not marry Nathaniel.'

'So it appears we are at an impasse,' he said, emitting a sigh. 'Do one thing for me, Rosalind. Pray for me?'

They gazed at one another for a long moment.

'You are not so much an enemy that I could not grant you that, Francis.'

She rose on tiptoes and kissed his cheek.

'God be with you.'

Before she could draw away he had caught her around her waist and gathered her against his body. His kiss released the emotions which neither up to that time had acknowledged in words. Rosalind felt a shudder run through him and without conscious thought she wound her arms around his neck, clasping him even closer. Reluctantly he slowly released her.

'If the Lord spares me, I will make one promise and that is to return here to you.'

With one last kiss he drew away and

disappeared into the shadows. He had not uttered one word of love, but hope surged within her, the hope that he would come back to her.

6

Rosalind was in the herb garden when she heard the pounding of hooves on the main driveway. She put down her gardening tools and pushed the damp strands of hair from her forehead, before hurrying into the house to see who had arrived in such haste.

Nathaniel was in the hall, receiving a despatch from a weary, dust-stained trooper whom Rosalind recognised as a member of Francis's troop.

'By all that is holy, this is excellent news!' Nathaniel exclaimed. 'Now we have Charles Stuart on the run!'

He glanced up to see Rosalind watching him.

'My dear, Trooper Lovell brings good news, of victory for the forces of Parliament! Yesterday, on the field of Naseby there was total defeat for the

King's army! Trooper Lovell rode through the night, on Major Latimer's orders to inform me of this important event.'

The colour drained from her face at the news of the Royalist defeat, but when Nathaniel mentioned Francis's name and the fact he was well, her whole being came alive.

Nathaniel walked towards her, a fanatical gleam in his black eyes.

'I wonder, will you still support that traitor, Charles Stuart, when I inform you that a cabinet, containing the Queen's letters to Charles, was captured on the battlefield. They stated that the King was plotting to bring over an Irish army against Parliament! Think of it, Rosalind, a Catholic army against his own subjects! Where are all your defiant words now in defence of that chief traitor?'

Rosalind realised he was attempting to goad her into retaliation, but today she would not rise to his bait. Without a word she walked from the hall.

Suddenly a huge wave of shame swept over her. While her thoughts were totally centred upon Francis, she had forgotten Thomas. He might have fought in the battle, perhaps having sustained a dreadful wound or worse! Was she so besotted with Francis, her own dear brother was excluded from her thoughts and prayers?

The following day, Nathaniel was away from the manor all afternoon. Darkness was falling as Rosalind entered the parlour, wondering what his errand was that kept him away for so many hours. William was lighting the candles and drawing the heavy brocade curtains when Nathaniel strode in.

'Leave us, steward,' he said in curt tones. 'See that supper is prepared quickly!' he added as William left the room.

The bland expression on the steward's face was a mask to hide the intense dislike he felt for Nathaniel Black. Rosalind was aware the whole household had no liking for the Puritan. Nathaniel moved to the fireplace and held out his hands to the welcoming warmth. Although it was the middle of June, the evenings were chilly. Several minutes of silence passed before he turned to face her.

'I have come to a decision, Rosalind. We must be married as soon as possible.'

She gasped audibly and rose to her feet.

'Why must we? I have made it quite clear that I am not ready for marriage, especially not to you!'

'Your consent is not a barrier to a union between us. I have already made the plans for the ceremony. We will be wed the day after the morrow.'

She stared at him, unable to comprehend how far his audacity reached.

'How dare you make arrangements without consulting me! You cannot control my life. You have my house and land, but you will never have me!'

'Oh, but you will marry me, Rosalind. You will stand by my side at the altar on the day I have chosen.'

'Then you will have to drag me there in chains, sir!' she cried in defiance.

'If that is the only way, then so be it,' he snapped. 'Your dowry must be released or the estate will be sold off to settle your debts!'

'If the house falls around me, I will not marry you!'

'You will come to me, willingly or not!' he snarled in a menacing tone, before striding to the door.

Rosalind felt as if her blood had turned to ice. His determination terrified her. She waited until Nathaniel was occupied eating his supper before she sought out William.

'I can scarce believe he could force you into marriage against your will,' William exclaimed in shocked tones.

'I cannot stay here, William. Surely there is somewhere I can go where he cannot find me.'

'My sister, Alice. She would be happy

to take you into her home. It would be the safest place for you to hide in Amersham.'

'Bless you, William. You are a true friend as well as a loyal servant, but I am afraid for your own safety. What if Nathaniel should ever discover your involvement in this?'

William shook his head, a look of calm assurance on his aged face.

'Master Black does not cause me any fear. Do not worry on my behalf.'

Despite William's assertion there was no cause for anxiety, Rosalind went to bed that night full of tension. She tossed and turned restlessly until the dawn light came. For the safety of her household, she had told no-one she intended leaving the manor, not even Mary.

William met her at the entrance to the orchard, holding Starlight's reins. He handed her a letter of explanation for his sister, Alice. After she had bade him farewell, Rosalind turned for a moment to look back at the house.

Her gaze swept for the last time over the only home she had ever known. In the early morning sunshine, the brick-work was a golden amber with dark green ivy clinging to the walls like a protective cloak.

With great effort, she shook off her deep sadness and led Starlight through the orchard and across the meadow. When she reached the path she took the opposite direction away from Ned Holden's smithy. She came to a crossroads and on a sudden impulse she decided to visit the Bell Inn in Chichester. The innkeeper there was the only person she knew who received news on the Royalist grapevine. It had been the favourite meeting place for Royalists, before the siege of the town crumbled and the area became overrun with Roundheads. She had often visited the landlord, Jim Woolley, to arrange when he would send the next Cavalier who needed a safe house to hide in.

She was unnerved to see several Parliamentary soldiers were hanging around the front entrance. Ignoring their stares, she dismounted and led her horse to the rear yard, where a stable lad took charge of Starlight. She entered the inn to see Jim Woolley had seen her arrival. He opened the parlour door and ushered her in.

'Come in here, Mistress Rosalind. We can talk in private. I've some good news for thee.'

'Is it about Thomas?' she asked eagerly once the door was closed.

'Aye, your brother is well and staying here,' Jim replied.

Relief flooded her to know Thomas was safe.

'Where is he? May I see him?'

'Steady on, Mistress Rosalind. Your brother left about a half hour since. 'Tis a wonder ye did not meet on the road.'

'I came a different route to my usual one, Jim. I only hope he does not go to the manor. He has sworn to settle a score with Nathaniel Black and he is hot-headed enough to do it!'

'Try not to think about it,' Jim tried

to reassure her. 'Ye'll see, Thomas will turn up later.'

'I cannot help but be anxious, Jim. If Thomas discovers Nathaniel is trying to force me into marriage with him, he will seek his death! May I stay here until Thomas returns? I was on my way to my steward's sister's house, but I can't leave now until I've seen Thomas.'

'Of course, mistress. I'll have a chamber prepared for your convenience and Bess will bring ye some refreshment.'

'Thank you, but later. I fear my stomach would not tolerate food at the moment. Thank you for your friendship, Jim.'

'Always remember, ye have friends here,' he assured her.

She was shown to a large, comfortable room on the upper floor with a view overlooking the garden. The rest of the morning was spent in agitation for Rosalind. How soon would Thomas return, she wondered. As each hour passed, her anxiety grew. She shared a midday meal with Jim and his wife, Bess, thankful to have their company. Shortly afterwards, Bess knocked on her door.

'Mistress, your brother is in the parlour! He's hurt quite bad!' she called.

Rosalind sprang up to open the door and sped down the stairs to the parlour. Thomas was stretched on a settle near the hearth when she entered. She felt faint when she saw the large red stain of blood on his shirt. Thomas gave her a weak smile.

'No need to look so alarmed. I had a little fracas with our friend, Nathaniel Black. He came out of it considerably worse, you will be glad to hear.'

Rosalind was horrified, all her fears realised.

'You should not have gone anywhere near the manor!'

Thomas's expression was grim.

'I had to show him who is the rightful owner. You would have expected no other of me!'

'Have you killed him?' she asked.

'There was no other choice, Ros. He attacked me first.'

He lay back on the settle, his face the colour of alabaster and there was no more strength left in him to speak. Rosalind knew they must stem the flow of blood quickly and get him to bed. Bess came in with a bowl of water and linen bandages. The gash across his chest was not as deep as they at first feared. Between them the two women cleaned his wound and applied healing salve. They bound the cloth strips tightly around his chest and helped him up the stairs.

Thomas leaned heavily on the two women as they moved slowly along the twists and turns of the old building. They came to what appeared to be a dead end, then Bess began to press on the wall with her fingers. A section of wall swung inwards to reveal a secret bedchamber.

The room they entered was windowless and small, but spotlessly clean and

114

there was fresh linen on the bed. It was well furnished and Rosalind guessed it must be the room where Jim hid the Royalists he helped.

'How very ingenious,' she remarked. 'No-one would ever guess there was another room here.'

'No-one but Jim and myself know about this room, mistress. We've hid many a King's man here lately.'

They helped Thomas into bed and Bess gave him a drink of mulled ale, containing herbs to deaden the pain. Rosalind gazed with anxiety at her brother. They would both go home now when Thomas was well again. She would defend the manor with her life, if need be!

7

The thought that Nathaniel was dead plagued Rosalind over the next few hours. Thomas had spent a comfortable night and his chest wound had stopped bleeding. She must return to the manor and discover the truth, if only for her own peace of mind. There was no alternative but to leave Thomas at the inn. Bess arranged for two of the tavern maids to look after him. Jim was doubtful of her decision to return home, but nothing could persuade Rosalind to change her mind.

'I have to return to the manor, Jim. If it is true that Nathaniel is dead, then my place is at home. When Thomas is well enough, he can join me.'

'Do I tell him where ye are?' Jim asked.

'No, or he will want to follow me. Tell

him I am visiting my steward's sister in Amersham.'

She was halfway home when she saw a troop of Cromwell's soldiers in the distance, heading in her direction. Feeling apprehensive, she quickly dismounted and led Starlight into the dense mass of trees by the roadside. Hidden, she waited until they passed. Mounting Starlight, she resumed her journey at a steady pace. Suddenly, she was brought to a shuddering halt when two mounted soldiers appeared from the trees and blocked her path.

'What do you want with me?' she asked, a wave of fear gripping her. 'Cannot an innocent traveller complete their journey without being accosted?'

'You may resume your journey when I receive some answers from you, Rosalind!'

The cold, authoritative voice behind her caused her to gasp and she swung round in the saddle.

'Francis!' she exclaimed, joy flaring within her, but it was quickly replaced by puzzlement when she saw there was no sign of welcome in his expression. 'I am glad to see you are well,' she said.

'I am well, Rosalind, thank you. I have survived to fight another day.'

She could not understand his hostile manner.

'Are you not glad to see me, Francis? Have you no word of greeting?'

'I cannot afford to waste time on niceties when my task is to bring to justice those who continually flout the laws of the land.'

Rosalind was stunned into silence by his curt reply. He was once again the cold, authoritative voice of Parliament and not the man who had expressed an earnest wish to return to her.

'Did you think we had not seen you go into the forest to hide? Why are you riding alone?' he asked. 'Don't you fear footpads? A lady such as yourself would be rich pickings in more ways than one!'

She felt the colour suffuse her face.

'I fear being accosted by Roundheads more!'

Francis ignored the acid comment. He issued an order to the two troopers to rejoin the rest of the group and they rode away swiftly.

'Say what you have to, Francis. I wish to reach the manor as soon as possible,' she said coldly.

'All I want are some answers to my questions. Tell me, have you seen your brother recently?'

Rosalind began to feel uneasy. She could not overlook the fact Francis was anti-royal and a traitor to her beliefs.

'No, I have not seen Thomas. If I had it would be none of your concern.'

'Oh, but it is, Rosalind. Thomas Pendrill is responsible for the murder of one of my troopers and now for attempted murder. I personally will ensure he is brought to justice.'

'He killed that trooper out of necessity. I know of no attempted murder you can accuse him of.'

'We both know he was at Pendrill

119

Manor yesterday.'

'How do you know? Did you see him?'

'No, but I visited the manor and spoke to the man he attempted to kill!'

He watched her reaction closely.

'Nathaniel lives?' she whispered in a shocked tone.

Francis's lips curved in grim amusement.

'Why surprised? Why should Nathaniel not be alive? But you thought your brother had done his task well and despatched him, did you not?'

'I will not admit to anything,' she replied coldly, wanting to kick herself for revealing so foolishly the fact she believed Nathaniel to be dead.

'Enough of this charade, Rosalind. I know your brother is wounded. Where is he?' he demanded.

She didn't answer, a lump forming in her throat.

'No matter, I will find him sooner or later,' he stated confidently.

'My brother's escape has festered

within you all this time, hasn't it?' she accused. 'You will not be satisfied until you see him hanged.'

'Believe what you will, but war makes demands that have to be met and personal feelings must be pushed aside.'

The eyes that swept over her were as bleak as a wintry sea.

'As you have pushed me aside,' she answered, her tone bitter.

'I will escort you to the manor. It is not safe for you to ride alone.'

Without further ado he took her reins and she had no choice but to let him lead Starlight. The remainder of the journey was accomplished in silence and when they arrived, she slid from Starlight's back without waiting for Francis to help her. He dismounted and caught hold of her arm as she was about to walk into the house.

'I would never harm you, Rosalind, but as I informed you once before whoever is found trying to destroy Parliament's aims, be it by murder or whatever, will be punished.'

'I am certain you will do your duty very efficiently, Major Latimer,' she said with sarcasm.

'I suggest you forget your war of words with me and go and make your peace with Nathaniel, before it is too late!'

'Is he dying?' she asked, raising startled eyes to him.

'There is very little possibility he will survive. Your brother did not intend that he should, did he?'

'I will go to him then,' she said, feeling subdued.

Francis still maintained his hold, preventing her from moving.

'Remember, Rosalind, you will be under close observation from now on!'

She subjected him to a look of pure hatred.

'I was a fool to believe I could ever trust a Roundhead!'

'We were both fools!' he shot back at her before releasing his grip and turning away to mount his horse.

She watched as he rode away and the

knowledge that their enmity was as strong as ever tore at her insides until she felt a physical pain. He had held her in his arms and though he had not spoken of love, he had given her cause to believe it would one day happen between them. Furthermore, he'd promised to return to her. It was obvious now the Parliamentary cause was more important to him than she was!

Nathaniel lay still, his eyes closed when she entered his chamber. Rosalind moved nearer to the bedside and stared down at him, noting his sunken cheeks and the ashen pallor of his skin. Looking at him now, she could not help but feel pity for him. Compassion would not allow her to gloat on his sorry state. He opened his eyes, aware of her presence.

'Rosalind, you have come back to me.'

His voice was barely above a whisper.

'No, Nathaniel. I have returned because this is my home, where I belong,' she told him not unkindly.

His bony fingers reached over the bedcovers towards her.

'Listen to me. Your brother will pay for his crimes,' he gasped, an effort to speak. 'I hope he rots in hell!'

'Nathaniel, make your peace with God, before it is too late!' she urged.

His fingers found her hand and gripped it with surprising strength.

'You belong to me, Rosalind. No-one else shall have you.'

With great effort he lifted his head from the pillow. A red stain appeared on the bandage around his chest. She pushed him down gently.

'You will never be rid of me, never.'

He closed his eyes. She stared at him, thinking he had died, then she realised he was still breathing. She left the bedchamber, chilled by his malevolent words. Did he intend to haunt her for ever?

The following morning, Rosalind awoke early after spending a disturbed night, mulling over Nathaniel's last words to her. He didn't appear to have any remorse for his actions, seemingly obsessed only with the thought of possessing her. She was leaving her bedchamber when she saw William walking towards her.

'Master Black passed away a few minutes ago,' he informed her in a quiet voice. 'He called your name several times and seemed distressed you were not there. I did not have time to awaken you before he died.'

'I am sorry I was not there at the last. It was the least I could do for him. He was my enemy, but I did not wish his death.'

'No-one will weep for him,' William stated without malice.

'I find that very sad,' Rosalind remarked. 'Everyone should have some-one who cares enough to weep over them.'

'I will attend to him, mistress, and inform Reverend Elliot to arrange the funeral service.'

'Thank you, William, but I fear our

troubles are not over. Major Latimer is determined to bring Thomas to account for Nathaniel's mortal wound. It appears I have exchanged one enemy for another.'

To contemplate Francis as her true enemy was unbearable. He was her only love. If he thrust a dagger into her heart, it would not alter the fact.

The morning of Nathaniel's funeral, two days later, was grey and dismal. Rosalind peered through the window panes, staring out at the inclement weather. She moved from the depressing scene outside to glance at her black-clad reflection in the mirror. The sombre colour accentuated the dark shadows under her eyes and the gown fitted more loosely than when she had worn it for her father's funeral. She picked up the heavy cloak.

The rain cleared and the sun began to break through the thinning clouds as Nathaniel was lowered into the earth. None of his relatives attended the funeral. Rosalind was aware it was because they would not enter a known Royalist household. However, several of his legal colleagues did attend, but even they rushed away afterwards, refusing Rosalind's offer of refreshment.

Later, Rosalind was alone in the parlour, sipping wine and reflecting upon all that had happened in the last few weeks. What would happen now concerning the manor? Who would be sent in place of Nathaniel, she wondered. Her house was still under sequestration and she did not think Parliament would allow her to live in her home without being under surveillance. Her thoughts were suddenly interrupted by heavy hammering on the main door. A minute later, William hurried in.

'Roundheads, mistress! A whole troop of them and they look as if they mean business!'

Outwardly she appeared calm, but inwardly she was sick with fear.

'Let them in, William. We have nothing to hide.'

William went to do her bidding. She followed him into the hall. Several soldiers knocked the steward aside as he opened the door and positioned themselves around the hall.

'What is the meaning of this?' she demanded.

The soldiers merely stared at her as though they hadn't heard.

'Are you all dumb? Where is your officer?'

'Here, Rosalind.'

The familiar voice caused her heart to lurch.

'I apologise for this intrusion.'

Francis stepped forward.

'What do you want with me? Nathaniel was buried barely three hours ago. I know you held little liking for him, but surely you could have some semblance of respect.'

His gaze swept over the abundance of her rich brown hair, shining with red tints. There was a momentary softening of regret in his flint grey eyes, but it was only fleeting and his mouth tightened with resolve.

'My apologies once again, Rosalind, but you leave me with no choice. If you had been honest with me as to the whereabouts of your brother, I would not be intruding on your privacy now!'

'My brother is not here. There is no cause to come bursting in armed to the teeth. Apart from my steward and a stable boy, we are all women. Has Cromwell waged war on us now? Give me one good reason for your action!'

Francis stared at her for a long moment before he turned to a trooper.

'Bring him in!' he commanded.

The trooper moved to obey and a minute later, Thomas was being pushed into the hall, a sword held to his back.

'Thomas!' Rosalind exclaimed, hurrying to him, recoiling when she saw the large blood stain on his shirt. 'How did they find you?'

'I was leaving the inn on my way here when they caught me.'

'Why didn't you stay hidden? They

would never have found you!' she berated him, then turned to Francis.

'My brother is bleeding! His wound must be attended to. He must rest!'

'Time to rest and recover so he may escape again?'

In that moment, Rosalind hated him almost as much as Nathaniel.

'Please, Francis,' she begged, 'just for a few days.'

Francis glanced at Thomas.

'Very well. Against my better judgement, he may remain here at the manor until he has recovered enough to travel, on one condition. You do not go near him.'

She was about to protest, then she saw the determination in his expression and agreed reluctantly to the condition. He ordered Thomas to be taken to a bedchamber and his wound attended to by the household maids. The remaining troopers were allowed to go to the kitchen for refreshment.

'Are you still intending to take Thomas for trial?' she asked, afraid her composure would crumble at any minute.

'It is what I have intended all along. Is there any reason I should change my mind?'

'Yes, Francis. You can save him by freeing him!'

She walked across the hall until she was standing so close, she had to raise her head to look into his face.

'Why should I do that, Rosalind?'

'For the sake of our past friendship, Francis,' she replied in a quiet voice.

'What was our past friendship, as you call it? Please remind me. I rather think it was too short for me to grant you favours now!'

'What do you want from me, Francis? To grovel on my knees before you? Will nothing I say or ask change your mind?'

The tortured questions poured out and she had to swallow hard as she realised how implacable he was. He did not answer and she began to turn away, deep misery lying heavy in her heart.

'Wait! I have not given you permission to leave yet!'

She spun round, full of indignation and was taken by surprise when he took quick strides towards her and caught her to him, his arms linking around her waist. She struggled to free herself.

'Have I a new master to replace Nathaniel, that you issue orders to me in my own home?' she challenged him.

'Be quiet,' he murmured, bending his head and claiming her lips before she could turn her head away.

There was no tenderness in his kiss, only, it seemed, a desire to subdue her into submission.

'Your soft lips are as tempting and willing as ever, Rosalind,' he said mockingly as she relaxed against him.

She raised her head, realising he was playing a game with her. Her arm moved swiftly towards his face, but he anticipated her intention and caught her hand.

'Before you try to sink your sharp, little claws into my face, listen to what I have to say. I will free your brother on one condition.'

He paused and watched her eyes light up with hope.

'The condition is that you first agree to marry me!'

His unexpected proposal took her completely by surprise. This time she knew it was no game he played.

8

'Marriage, to you? You are insane to even suggest it!' she said and dismissed the unexpected proposal from her mind as she spoke.

'Come now, Rosalind, the idea of marriage to me cannot be abhorrent to you. After all, you were contemplating marriage to Nathaniel!'

'I will not be forced into marriage with anyone. Nathaniel was attempting to do so to release my dowry and save the estate and I was determined to withstand him. I will do the same with you.'

'At the expense of your brother's life? I think not. We are not discussing bricks and mortar now. I am a wealthy landowner and I will pay the debts owing on this estate for your sake only. I want none of your dowry.'

He released her and drew back.

'Forget your pride, Rosalind, for the sake of your brother or he could end up on the execution block. Cromwell will not tolerate continued rebellion and murder.'

'Murder?' she scoffed. 'How can you speak of murder when your troops murder innocent people every day?'

'Horrendous deeds are always justified in time of war, Rosalind. We are all guilty, one way or another. To get back to my proposal, will you marry me in exchange for your brother's freedom?'

'Why are you insisting on marriage as a bargaining point in freeing Thomas? There is nothing but hatred between us.'

His eyes betrayed nothing of his thoughts.

'I do not need to give you a reason now. Fulfil your part of the bargain and I will release your brother.'

'Very well, Francis, I will marry you, but only when Thomas has recovered and is a long way from here,' she said in a determined tone.

'It will be as you say,' he agreed.

He turned away from her and, feeling dismissed, she moved to the staircase. Halfway up she turned to look at him and saw, in that unguarded moment, how strained and weary he appeared. Her own unhappiness gave way to such a feeling of love for him she was tempted to try and bridge the insurmountable gulf between them. His words which floated up to her, however, dashed that hope instantly.

'By the way, Rosalind, there will be a trooper watching your every move from now on.'

The remark was hurtful, but she chose not to reply and continued ascending the stairs. He had promised to pay the estate debts, but it was not that alone which had lifted her spirits. In her wildest dreams she had imagined walking to the altar to become Francis' wife. Now it was going to happen, she knew she would rather be bound to him in enmity, than not have him at all.

★ ★ ★

Six weeks passed and in all that time, Rosalind was not allowed to see Thomas. She had to rely on daily reports from Mary, who gave her messages from him. He was recovering well, a fact she was thankful for, but knew there would come a time when he must leave the manor.

Eventually the day did arrive when Thomas was well enough to take his departure. Rosalind was at last allowed to see him. Her heart constricted when she saw there was none of his usual exuberance, only a subdued resignation in the dull eyes that looked at her. She fought hard to keep back her tears.

'Where will you go, Tom?' she asked.

'I'm taking a ship to the low countries, until the war is over. My fighting days are finished. This wound has weakened me more than I thought.'

'Holland! It is so far away!' she exclaimed in dismay.

He put his arms around her in a

137

comforting manner. They were both well aware it could be many years before they met again.

'Much better to be free in Holland than languishing in prison, eh? There is one thing I find puzzling though. Why has Latimer allowed me to go free? What does he gain by it?'

His glance went to the Roundhead, standing at the far end of the hall watching them.

'He has done it out of friendship for me, Tom,' she replied quietly.

'Friendship with him, a traitor? Are you out of your mind?' he exclaimed incredulously, his eyes sparking with anger.

'Please just accept the fact, Tom. Francis is a man to be respected. He is not in the same mould as Nathaniel was.'

She sought to reassure him, but the doubts she possessed did not put her own mind at rest so easily.

★　★　★

Rosalind moved across to the mirror and stared at her reflection. The velvet and satin gown in pale green was a good choice and Mary had painstakingly sewn pearls into the bodice. In the mirror, she could see Mary, sniffing into a kerchief, and she turned to thank the girl for her hard work in preparing the gown so quickly.

'I am not going to my doom, Mary. Dry your eyes. I want my maid to look her prettiest today.'

' 'Tis you who will be the prettiest today and rightly so,' the maid remarked, drying her eyes.

'I do hope I am not making the biggest mistake of my life, Mary.'

'If there is one thing I'm sure of, it's that you are doing the right thing in marrying the major, Roundhead or not. He is a good man.'

Rosalind studied the girl thoughtfully. Mary was a good judge of character and sounded confident. She wished she could share her confidence.

Rosalind's heeled shoes tapped on

the stone flags as she walked down the church aisle, holding on to William's arm. Francis was waiting at the altar and he turned as she approached. The gaze that swept from her head to her feet was enigmatic. Throughout the ceremony, whenever she glanced at him, his profile appeared to be cast in stone and not once did he smile.

Was he regretting his decision, she wondered. At last it was over and Francis was drawing her arm through his own and leading her from the cold confines of the church, into the warmth of the sunshine. Rosalind took in deep breaths of the fresh air. She turned to look at her husband and saw he was gazing at her with a tender expression which both surprised and embarrassed her.

'You have never looked so radiant as you do today, my beautiful wife,' he whispered in a husky voice, his eyes moving over her face and hair.

He was about to speak again, but Reverend Elliot came over to offer his congratulations and the moment was gone. He did not attempt to resume the conversation and they walked back to the house in silence.

The wedding feast was set out on the long table in the hall and during the meal, William hovered nearby, serving the wine. Rosalind was amazed at the deference her steward showed towards Francis. William detested all Roundheads, but here it seemed was one who had won his respect. Francis reached out and touched her cold hand.

'You seem unhappy, Rosalind. Are you already regretting your decision to marry me?'

'We made a bargain and I do not go back on my word. I think you now owe me an explanation as to why marriage was your bargaining point.'

'Yes, it is time you know the truth. The manor was shortly to have a new administrator and I was not the one the authorities had in mind. I know the man chosen and he is every bit as inflexible and intolerant as Nathaniel, believe me. I informed them we were about to be married and they agreed, in the circumstances, I take charge of the estate.'

Her eyes widened in anger and she rose to her feet, but Francis dragged her down into her seat again.

'This was all planned, wasn't it? As soon as you became aware Nathaniel wouldn't live, you acted quickly to step into his shoes. Your ambitions are as despicable as his were and even more so because I judged you to be a man of integrity!'

His expression darkened.

'Whatever you may believe, I do not covet this estate. I have given you a true and justifiable account of what was about to take place.'

'Justifiable in your eyes maybe!' she hissed.

'Don't turn from my friendship, Rosalind. I have no desire to see you dispose of your home. I informed the authorities you have severed your previous connections with the Royalist cause, to save you further harassment.'

'You have told them what?' she exclaimed, turning fierce burning eyes to him. 'You had no right to! I see only too clearly that you seek to use me as a pawn to further your own political ambitions.'

She gave a brittle laugh.

'I can hear them now, gloating that the little Royalist upstart of Pendrill Manor has been tamed at last by Major Latimer. One more malignant stronghold subdued!'

Tears welled in her eyes and she sprang to her feet before he could prevent her. She hurried from the hall into the parlour, oblivious of the bemused faces of the troopers at the table. Francis followed her and closed the parlour door from prying eyes. He strode towards her and twisted her around to face him, his fingers digging painfully into her shoulders.

'You little fool!' he rasped. 'I am only thinking of you! Do you want another Nathaniel here to dominate your life?'

'Are you not in the same mould, seeking to dominate me? Will I be any happier with you as my master?' she replied, with a note of resignation.

She suddenly felt too weary of it all to fight any longer.

'Oh, Rosalind, will it be so terrible to be my wife? All I want is your happiness,' he answered, his own anger gone.

'Whatever it will be like, Francis, nothing can alter the fact I am your wife. We have our whole lives to regret it!'

He sighed in exasperation, before he turned on his heel and strode from the room without another word.

Rosalind was in her bedchamber, later that evening, staring at the jewelled wedding ring on her finger. The rubies shone with a rich lustre in the flicking candlelight, almost mocking her and she hastily pulled it from her finger. She was disrobing when there came a light tap on the door.

Francis entered and smiled wryly as she jumped to her feet and subjected him to a sullen expression. He crossed the room and caught a strand of her unbound hair. His hand touched the bare skin of her shoulder and the contact was like fire meeting fire.

'Are you afraid of me?' he asked.

'Have I cause to fear you, Francis?'

She raised her clear gaze to his. He smiled enigmatically.

'Perhaps, when I hold you in my arms and melt the barrier of ice you protect yourself with.'

She blushed at the intimate visions his words invoked.

'It will never happen,' she said resolutely. 'Do you think I would bed with you when I am aware of your devious moves to obtain my brother's estate and wealth?'

Anger turned his eyes to steel.

'Ours will be a true marriage, Rosalind. I have kept my part of the bargain by freeing your brother, now you must keep yours!'

'I detest you more than I did Nathaniel!'

Her voice was full of loathing, but goaded by her haughty manner, he dragged her to him, claimed her lips and kissed her with an intensity which hurt. She struggled until his passionate anger froze and he lifted his head.

'I will prove you do not hate me!' he said, with arrogant confidence.

He drew her close again and buried his face in the soft cloud of her hair. His burning kisses scorched a trail across her face and down to the low neckline of her chemise. Unable to think coherently, she began to weaken. When he held her like this she had no defence against his magnetism and to yield would be so easy.

'Why don't you admit this is what you want?' he whispered.

Rosalind felt she was drowning in a sea of longing.

'Not like this, Francis,' she pleaded. 'Not without love. Take me if you will, but it will be by force!'

He became still and drew away, a chilling expression contorting his features into a cold mask.

'You need have no fears. I would not stoop so low that I would rape my own wife! You may lock your door from now on. I no longer have any desire to come near you!'

The look he gave her was one of utter contempt before he strode to the door. He turned and raked her trembling form with a bleakness shadowing his eyes.

'I will find my pleasures elsewhere, if I must. All I ask is that you act the dutiful wife when we entertain guests. I am sure that is not beyond your capabilities! Good-night, Rosalind.'

The loud slam of the door reverberated throughout the quiet household. Rosalind stared at it for long minutes, unable to control the severe pain that had seized her. She had completely annihilated Francis and destroyed for ever any truce which may have developed between them.

In the days which followed, Rosalind sank deeper into depression and loneliness, wondering if she could endure the course her life had taken. Francis ignored her as much as possible, taking his meals with the troopers. Often at night, as she lay in bed, the sounds of laughter in the hall would torment her with the vision of him turning his threat into reality and finding another woman to give him solace. She was only too aware it was entirely her fault he was not there at her side as he should be. She reached the conclusion it would be up to her to make the first move towards a reconciliation. She could not live in the same house without some kind of truce and she resolved, at the first opportunity, to seek him out.

The next day, Francis and the troop rode out early and were still away when darkness was falling. A state of apprehension filled Rosalind at the delay in confronting Francis. Her heart began to beat faster when at last she heard their arrival in the courtyard.

Should she attempt to speak to him now? She decided after a long day's ride he would not be in a receptive frame of mind to listen to her, but she could not delay too long or her courage would desert her.

An hour later, after the troopers had settled and fed their horses, they gathered in the hall to eat their evening meal. Taking a deep breath, Rosalind made her way downstairs and, reaching the hall, stood there, undecided, as Francis was nowhere to be seen. She was about to turn and go back to her bedchamber when her glance went to the open parlour door. Something within her died at the sight which greeted her shocked gaze. Francis was locked in a passionate embrace with a fair-haired woman!

Rosalind was rooted to the spot and could not tear her gaze away. Anguish tore through her, but still she could not move. Francis lifted his head and said something which caused the woman to laugh. Rosalind had to admit she was beautiful, but there was a hardness in the painted features, smiling up at Francis in a provocative way.

She sped back up the stairs. Once in the privacy of her room, she fell on to the bed in utter despair and rejection. It was too late to attempt a reconciliation. Her senseless enmity had driven Francis into the arms of another woman, as he'd threatened. Who could blame him? Her pride, the one thing she had held on to, was as useless now as her love for Francis.

9

The sign of the Bell Inn creaked noisily in the strengthening wind. A faint glow came from one of the hostelry windows and Rosalind began to knock on the stout, wooden door as hard as she could. Presently it was opened to her insistent hammering by Jim Woolley.

'Why mercy me, Mistress Rosalind!' he exclaimed. 'Whatever are ye doing out abroad at this ungodly hour?'

Without waiting for her reply, he ushered her in along the passage to the parlour. The elderly innkeeper eyed her with fatherly concern as he indicated she seat herself on a padded settle.

'I am so sorry for bursting in on you at this hour, Jim. Could you provide me with a room for the night?'

'Now, now, Mistress Rosalind, ye are always welcome to stay here whenever ye wish.'

Gratitude formed a lump in Rosalind's throat. She was aware how many times Jim and Bess had risked their lives, hiding Cavaliers at the inn and putting themselves in danger when they were caring for Thomas.

'I have good news, Jim. Thomas has made a full recovery and Major Latimer has allowed him to go free, at my request.'

'The saints be praised, mistress, that be splendid news.'

The relief was evident on Jim's rotund face.

'The bad news is, Thomas has gone to the low countries for the duration of the war. He feels he cannot fight for the cause as he once did, before he sustained his wound.'

'I be sorry to hear that, but a man like your brother cannot stand idly by knowing he is useless to fight for his king.'

'Thomas's release was not unconditional, Jim.'

She paused, wondering what his

reaction was going to be on hearing she had married a Roundhead.

'I consented to marry Major Latimer in exchange for Thomas's freedom. We were married two weeks ago.'

Jim's expression turned to astonishment.

'You are wed to a Roundhead? Well, I never would have believed it!'

He saw the expression on Rosalind's face and was immediately contrite.

'I'm not judging ye, lass. Ye have thine own reasons, I'm sure.'

'I did not intend for you to become involved, Jim, but he may come here searching for me, when he discovers I have run away. I am travelling to my steward's sister's home, but I am afraid to travel during darkness.'

'Just tell me one thing,' Jim asked gently. 'Why did ye run away? Was he cruel to ye?'

'Oh, no, he has never been unkind to me. He has used me, as Nathaniel did, to gain control of the manor. I thought he was more honourable, but it appears I was wrong.'

'War does strange things to folk, mistress. Sometimes we are powerless to prevent their actions. Now, let's arrange a room for ye and Bess will get ye a bite to eat.'

When Jim had gone to prepare her room, she began to reflect on the complicated turn her life had taken in recent weeks. Several emotions warred together in her mind — anger, misery, humiliation, but the overriding one of all was her love for Francis. Not even the memory of him in that other woman's arms could destroy her love.

Running away, she knew, would not resolve the situation and she could not hope to hide from him for ever, but to remain in the same house had become intolerable.

Bess entered at that moment with a tray of food. Although Rosalind did not feel like eating, the innkeeper's wife persuaded her to eat a small portion of bread and cheese and drink some warm ale, laced with honey and cinnamon.

Rosalind began to feel sleepy and she was glad to follow Bess to the upper chamber she was to occupy for the night. She was so weary she hardly had the strength to remove her shoes and gown before tumbling into bed and drifting immediately into a deep sleep.

The next thing she knew, Bess was standing by her bed, shaking her.

'Mistress Rosalind, wake up!'

There was great urgency in her voice. Rosalind lifted her head from the pillow to see the grey light of dawn filtering through the shutters.

'Roundheads, outside in the yard. You must hurry and hide in the secret room, in case 'tis you they are looking for!' Bess urged.

In a daze, Rosalind got out of bed and quickly collected her clothing.

'Quick as you can, mistress!'

Bess picked up the candlestick and Rosalind followed her along the twists and turns of the old building until they came to the end of the passage where the secret room was. Bess opened the panel and they entered the tiny bedchamber.

'I must go now. Bolt the panel after me.'

Bess squeezed Rosalind's hand reassuringly.

'Don't worry, you'll be safe in here and there is plenty of fresh air coming in through a vent in the wall. I must go and tidy your chamber in case the Roundheads start searching.'

She left Rosalind with the lighted candle and a spare one and went out. Left alone, Rosalind settled herself on the bed and pulled the heavy coverlet over her. In the distance, she could hear footsteps thumping up the stairs. Several doors were opened and slammed. The footsteps were very close now, so close she could hear the troopers calling to each other, then they were moving away until there was only silence.

Rosalind expelled her breath in relief. Then began the agonising wait for Bess to come and tell her she could leave her hiding place. After what seemed an interminable time she could not endure her imprisonment a minute longer. She quietly slid back the panel bolt and crept along the passage. At the head of the stairs she hesitated. The silence was eerie. Why wasn't there the usual noise of a busy hostelry? Why hadn't Bess come to tell her the soldiers had gone? Gathering her courage she began to descend the creaking stairs.

The door to the parlour was wide open and she could see on the table there was food set out, a loaf of bread, various savoury pies, cheese and fruit. Rosalind's stomach protested at the sight. She entered the room and walked to the table. The door behind her crashed to with such force she spun round in terror. Too late she realised she had walked into a trap!

There was triumph in Francis's flint grey eyes and a mocking smile on his lips as he moved into the centre of the room. Rosalind glanced round, but there was no way out, short of trying to pit her strength against his far superior one. Of course, he must have been alerted to her coming when she trod on the creaking stairs.

'I knew you would emerge, sooner or later. It was worth the waiting. The time for running and hiding is over, Rosalind.'

He advanced slowly towards her.

'What have you done with Bess and Jim? Where are they?'

'They are quite safe, being looked after by my troopers, far enough away so they couldn't warn you.'

'I am surprised you thought I was worthy of your concern, that you hunt me down like this. Is your pride dented, Francis?'

'You are my wife, Rosalind,' he stated quietly.

'I am your possession,' she said. 'How did you know I was here?'

'I didn't. I have a traveller to thank for being so observant and remembering seeing a finely-dressed woman on a white horse, heading in this direction. I only had to look in the stable here and find the white horse which would lead me to the lady I sought. I think you owe me an explanation as to why you departed the manor in such seemly haste.'

'I do not have to explain to you why I think our marriage is a farce,' she said haughtily. 'I cannot see any reason for remaining a minute longer in the same house as yourself!'

'Who made the marriage a farce? You scorned the marriage bed, not I. At least tell me why you hate me so much, apart from the fact of my being a Roundhead.'

She stared into his eyes, which at that moment showed some bewilderment. She felt a sense of relief that at last she could unburden herself.

'Very well, I will tell you. Nathaniel said many cruel things which hurt me and he was also going to force me into marriage against my wishes, but he did not bring women to the manor and openly indulge with them. If you must

159

commit adultery, can you not do it away from our home?'

The puzzled expression his face cleared, then he began to laugh.

'Now I begin to understand why you ran like a frightened rabbit. It wasn't hate that drove you away, but sheer jealousy!'

Rosalind was stunned into silence as she faced the truth.

'It must have been Lettie you saw at the manor. She is a singer and came to entertain the men. She is not interested in sharing my bed and neither do I want her to, but she does like to flirt.'

He eyed Rosalind in amusement, taking in her stony expression.

'I can well imagine what visions your jealous little mind must have conjured up!'

'Nothing could be further from the truth,' she snapped. 'You are mad to believe I am jealous of your tavern wenches!'

'Whatever is the truth, dear wife, our union is as valid as any other and will remain so!'

The firmness in his tone sent a shiver of apprehension through her.

'There is too much bitterness between us, for me ever to be a true wife to you, Francis.'

'The fact was made very plain to me on our wedding night,' he said wryly. 'I made it perfectly clear to you I would not make demands where they are not welcome. I am sorry if you misunderstood Lettie's intentions. Believe me, I would never flaunt other women in your home, or anywhere.'

She stared into the sombre depths of his eyes, longing to believe him.

'Come home with me, Rosalind,' he urged. 'Let us try to live together as amicably as we can. I don't want to force you to accompany me, but I will if you persist in this foolishness.'

'If I am forced against my will to return home, then the situation will only be worse and even more intolerable for me.'

'Do you detest me so much that a

house as large as Pendrill Manor cannot accommodate us both adequately?'

'I married you, Francis, solely so my brother could obtain his freedom. Is that not enough reason for you?'

Raw anger flared in his eyes and he took a step nearer to her. Rosalind backed away.

'You know it is not enough, Rosalind! You are my wife and I want our marriage to be a true one.'

He moved even nearer and she took a step backwards again. An oak dresser brought her to a halt, trapping her.

'I can never fulfil the rôle of a wife. Please do not ask it of me.'

He reached out and touched her cheek gently.

'Do you wish to live a lifetime of loneliness, Rosalind?' he whispered.

A tremor ran through her body and the old desire for him surged within her, leaving her weak and defenceless. He bent his head and though she knew he was about to kiss her, she could not move, did not want to move as the pressure of his arms tightened around her waist, drawing her to him. Very gently his lips touched her own.

'There need be no hatred between us, sweet Rosalind,' he murmured.

The craving for his touch and the tenderness of his kiss began to disarm her, opening the floodgates of love. For those few brief moments in his arms she was sent spiralling heavenward.

'Your lips tell me you desire me as much as I do you. I believe you ran away just to gain my attention.'

The arrogance in his tone brought Rosalind resurfacing from the depths of desire as if cold water had been thrown in her face. She tried to push herself from his arms.

'What else has your arrogance deduced, Francis? That I am totally besotted with you? Allow me to inform you, that you are entirely wrong!'

'Enough of your foolishness, Rosalind.'

He kept a vice-like hold upon her waist.

'I want you by my side and however much you protest, I think you want that also.'

'It is only your pride which concerns you. I mean nothing to you!'

She was determined not to give in to his demands. Desperate to escape, she put her hands behind her on the dresser and felt for any hard object. Her fingers touched a candlestick and without thinking sanely, she lifted up the heavy metal object and brought it crashing down with a sickening thud on the side of his head! The blow stunned him and she watched, horrified, as he reeled backwards, blood beginning to trickle from the gash on his temple. She dropped the candlestick and ran!

10

Rosalind reached the summit of a hill and gazed around at the strange, hostile landscape. The scene was suddenly lit with a jagged fork of lightning and huge spots of rain began to fall. Minutes later, the heavens opened. Her cloak was soon drenched and she felt hungry and miserable. In her panic to escape, she'd missed the turning to Amersham. Now she was hopelessly lost and could not hope to get her bearings in this storm.

What had possessed her to strike out at Francis so viciously? What had she achieved by running away? Was it his arrogant pride which had sent him out scouring the countryside for her or was it because he truly cared for her?

In the valley below, she could see a black huddle of buildings. Surely there was someone who would give her shelter. She urged Starlight down the steep hillside, but her relief turned to dismay when she neared the collection of cottages and realised it was an abandoned village. Several of the buildings were falling into ruin, but as she rode on, one or two of the cottages still appeared in a reasonable state.

She dismounted outside the one that looked the most habitable, grateful that at least it would offer shelter from the elements. She longed for the comforting warmth of a fire to melt the stiffness in her muscles. Anxious to shelter from the rain, she pushed open the wooden door and was astounded to see a clean, tidy interior. The few items of furniture, a table, two chairs and a bed set against one wall, gave evidence it was occupied. A fire burned low in the hearth and, drenched to the bone, Rosalind moved over to its heat. There was only the one room and she wondered where the occupant was. Surely they would not deny hospitality to her.

Then she remembered poor Starlight, left out in the rain. Reluctantly, she left the cosy room, hoping there would be some sort of stable for her horse. Leading Starlight around to the rear of the cottage, she was relieved to see what looked like a barn with a hole in the roof. Surprisingly it was equipped with straw and hay. She quickly dried the creature down, ensuring she was well away from the hole in the roof and left her munching some hay.

Well, at least Starlight was fed for the night, she thought, not having found any food for herself in the cottage. She lay on the bed, waiting for the occupant to return and listened to the rolling thunder breaking overhead. At last it moved on until she could hear only a distant rumble. She grew steadily more drowsy and very soon fell asleep.

She was brought to rude wakefulness by the door being flung wide open. She had no time to do anything but stare at the man framed in the doorway. They both stared at each other in amazement.

'By all the gods, what have we here? I think my prayers for a wench to keep me warm this night have been answered!'

Rosalind noted his wealthy attire and cultured tones, but she was immediately wary of his bold statement and insolent stare. She sprang off the bed and backed against the wall, wishing she could get the small dagger which was in her saddlebag on the floor.

'Sir, forgive my intrusion, but I have become lost and wanted shelter until the storm had passed over.'

He moved towards her and she tensed with fear, but he walked to the fire and turned his back to it to subject her to keen scrutiny.

'Come, extract yourself from that wall and sit here, near the fire. I do not intend hurting you.'

Warily, Rosalind did as he bid and sat on one of the rickety chairs.

'May I introduce myself?'

He smiled and seated himself on the other chair.

'My name is Miles Kesteven and I have been using this hovel as a shelter for several weeks now. It has served my purpose well, even though the comforts are few.'

He cast a disapproving glance around the room. She began to relax. He had an open, friendly face and an air of cheerful optimism in his manner.

'I must admit, a pigsty would have been preferable to being out in that storm,' she remarked ruefully.

Miles' pale blue eyes roamed over her face and hair in an appreciative way.

'A pigsty would definitely not be a suitable haven for someone as lovely as you, mistress.'

'Why are you staying here?' she asked. 'Are you a Royalist and hiding from the Roundheads?'

A shutter drew across Miles' features and his smile faded.

'Why should you want to know that, unless you are a . . . '

He didn't finish the sentence. Both heard the approach of horses. He sprang to the window.

'Roundheads!'

He turned to look at Rosalind.

'No-one ever passes this way. Could they be looking for you?'

If it was Francis's troop searching for her, they must not find her! And, if Miles was a Royalist, he would not wish to be seen either.

'It is possible they are looking for me. My husband may have sent out a patrol for that purpose.'

Miles' took in the quality of her gown and a thought entered his head.

'If the Roundheads are hopeful of finding you, perhaps I may have a way of securing a safe passage for myself.'

'What are you going to do?'

A shiver of fear ran through her when he grasped her arm tightly. He extinguished the fire by stamping on the embers with his boot.

'I am a Royalist, as I suspect you are yourself. I have no love for the

Roundheads!' she cried, trying to pull away, but he was already dragging her through the rear door into the damp yard.

'You are married to one. That gives me enough reason not to trust you!'

His voice turned from good-natured banter to suspicious wariness. His grip on her arm was like iron pincers and suddenly she began to wish she was safe at home. Home! The word seemed to thrust itself into her being in mockery and she suddenly realised what a fool she was. She loved Francis and her place was by his side.

'What good am I to you?' she asked.

'I may have to use you as a bargaining point,' he muttered.

His features held grim determination as he pushed her towards the barn.

'What are you intending to do?' she asked.

'Ride far away from here and you will accompany me.'

Rosalind tried again to free herself from his grasp.

'Leave me here, please. You can travel swifter without me.'

Miles chuckled mockingly.

'Do you take me for a fool? Leave you here to send a pack of rebels on my tail?'

'I may be the wife of a Roundhead officer, but I remain true to the King's cause. I would never betray you, I swear on my life.'

He mulled over her statement.

'Can it be possible to yield to a traitor and still be a loyal subject of His Majesty?'

'I love my husband, but that would not prevent me laying down my life for my king.'

The clamour of voices cut into their conversation. Rosalind turned to see Francis and the troopers, spilling into the yard. Francis advanced towards them, his sword drawn ready. Relief flooded through her to know he had come searching for her.

'We wondered where your hiding place was, Kesteven. You were very careless riding out in full daylight.'

Rosalind's heart sank. Francis hadn't been searching for her after all. She suddenly didn't care what happened to her. She stared at Francis with dull eyes and was taken by surprise when Miles moved with the speed of light and dragged her against his body, his arm around her neck.

'Tell your men to back away or I harm the lady!'

The steely determination in Miles' voice left Rosalind in no doubt he meant every word he had said. She shivered with terror.

'Harm her and I will kill you myself!' Francis replied with the same iron-hard resolve.

'Is he your husband?' Miles asked, close to her ear.

'Yes,' she croaked, the pressure of his arm preventing her from speaking clearly.

'Get rid of your men, now!' Miles demanded, backing towards the barn, dragging Rosalind with him.

Francis gave a curt command and the troopers backed away. His features were set like granite as he surveyed the Cavalier.

'I will make a bargain with you, Roundhead,' Miles shouted across the yard. 'I go free, unmolested by your soldiers, and the lady is yours.'

'And if I do not agree to your terms?' Francis asked, with a thread of menace in his tone.

'Then I carry out my threat to harm her. Think carefully, Roundhead, my words are not idly spoken.'

'Very well, collect your horse and go before I am tempted to plunge this sword into your heart!'

Francis's voice was lined with steel. Miles released Rosalind and pushed her towards the horses.

'Get my horse and be quick. I do not trust this husband of yours!'

Rosalind hurried to do as he bid, but as she began to lead Miles' horse from the barn, he moved quickly towards her and, grasping her around her waist, lifted her high into the saddle, then he swung himself up behind her and kicked the horse into movement. Francis, realising he had been outwitted, tried to grab the reins as the horse sped by, but received a blow from Miles' boot in his chest and he was knocked to the ground.

Rosalind struggled to no avail. Miles held her firm, urging the horse into a gallop. The shouts of the soldiers carried in the air as they set off in pursuit. The area was covered by dense woodland and very soon Miles had directed his mount into the dark refuge of a wood. Here, he dismounted and pulled Rosalind roughly from the saddle.

'You broke your promise!' she cried, infuriated by his deceit. 'I am no use to you and will only hinder your chance of escape! Please allow me to return to my husband.'

'No! You stay with me. If you are the Royalist you profess to be, then you will not mind when I kill that Roundhead husband of yours!'

The cold, calculating purpose in his voice terrified her.

'There is a dozen men at least in his troop. You cannot kill them all!'

'Watch and witness, my beauty, for here they come.'

Miles reached out for her and fastened his hand tightly across her mouth. She could hear the troopers milling about at the edge of the trees and Francis giving orders to split into groups. Unable to shout out, the only weapon she had was her foot and she used it to good effect on Miles' leg. He uttered an oath and momentarily loosened his grip on her. She fled, shouting Francis's name, conscious of Miles' heavy footsteps thundering after her. He caught her and pushed her to the ground.

'Francis!' she screamed, hearing the rasping sound of Miles' sword as he withdrew it.

'He cannot save you now, Round-head whore!' he muttered.

She saw the flash of his sword scything down towards her and had the presence of mind to roll away. She could not hope to evade his murderous intentions a second time and she lay, waiting for death!

'Rosalind!'

Her heart somersaulted at the sound of Francis calling her name as he came thrashing through the undergrowth in a fury to confront the Cavalier.

'Where are your men?' Miles sneered. 'Why do you not call on them to aid you?'

Francis advanced, his sword held ready.

'I have no need of them to deal with you, malignant.'

His glance strayed to Rosalind.

'Are you hurt?'

She struggled to her feet.

'No, I am unharmed.'

'Good, now go and seek my troopers. They will care for you until I have dealt with this scoundrel.'

'Be careful, Francis!' she called,

before stumbling away to find the troopers and warn them their officer was about to fight the Royalist.

Steel was already clashing against steel in the still air as she ran, calling for help. The troopers heard her call and had soon regrouped around her. Several went to the aid of Francis, but the fight was already over. Miles lay on the ground, blood seeping from a gash in his shoulder.

'Take this man and keep him under guard,' Francis ordered. 'Unfortunately he will live when that wound is tended, but he will receive appropriate punishment in due course!'

Miles was led away, holding his hand to the wound to try to stem the flow. Francis wiped the Cavalier's blood from his sword and re-sheathed it. He walked to where his horse waited and gave orders for the troopers to go on ahead to the manor with the prisoner. Rosalind followed in silence, wondering what she should say to Francis. Was he willing to forgive her foolish action in dealing him the blow on his head, or was it all too late? He did not speak for a moment and she cringed when her gaze went to the congealed wound on his temple.

'Thank you, Francis, for coming to my aid,' she said in a quiet voice. 'That man treated me kindly at first, but just before you came, he had no compunction about attempting to kill me.'

'This is the last time I scour the countryside for you, Rosalind. You have shown me only too plainly what is your opinion of me. I give you your freedom. Tell me where you wish to go and I will escort you there.'

Rosalind felt her heart was being ripped in two at his curt words. If she did not speak now the moment would be lost for ever.

'I wish to go home, Francis, with you, to Pendrill Manor.'

A deep sigh escaped him.

'I seem to remember this is what we were discussing when I received this.'

His hand went to his temple.

'What has changed?'

'I have, Francis. I am truly sorry for what I did to you. There was no justification for such action.'

'I accept your apology, but it still does not alter the state of our marriage.'

His tone was hostile.

'I think it better for both of us to have this marriage annulled. It will not present any problem as it has not been consummated. Come, now is not the time to discuss this issue.'

He held out his hand to help her mount his horse.

'I do not want our marriage annulled, Francis,' she said, placing her cold hand in his.

She had spoken in a low voice and he wondered if he'd heard aright.

'I want to be your wife in every sense of the word,' she added.

His grip on her hand tightened.

'Do you realise what you are saying? Once we take that final, irrevocable step, there can be no annulment.'

'I have never been so certain of what

I am saying, Francis. I love you, I always have and it is only my own petty jealousy which has kept us apart. Will you forgive me for hurting you? I panicked, thinking you would force me to return to the manor with you.'

Surprising her, he raised his hands to her hair and began to smooth out the silken tangles.

'Yes, you hurt me, but I was hurt more inside by the thought you hated me so much you could not bear the idea of me touching you, let alone living with me. The fault is not all yours. We have both been foolish in our turn. I love you, Rosalind, and there was never a moment, deep down, when I did not. Forgive me for being so harsh towards you.'

He drew her close and enfolded her in his arms.

'I forgive you and more, but tell me, Francis, was it me you were searching for and not Miles?'

'It is true we've been on the look-out for Kesteven for many weeks. He's been acting as a Royalist spy, but there was only one person on my mind this day and that is you, my love. It was sheer luck we saw him and followed him here without his knowledge. I couldn't believe it when I found you with him.'

'Tell me why . . . ' Rosalind began to speak.

He put his finger to her mouth.

'Not now, my love. Time enough for questions and explanations,' he said gently. 'We are both tired and hungry and I want to take you home before you decide to disappear again.'

Rosalind gave a sigh of happiness as she snuggled close to the comforting warmth of his body. Yes, she thought, they had all the time in the world to make matters right between them. Francis lifted Rosalind on to his horse and swung himself up behind her, then he turned his mount back in the direction of the village to collect Starlight.

They were nearing the village when clouds began to gather and the rain began to fall steadily again. When they reached the cottage, Rosalind went inside to shelter while Francis led his horse round the back to the makeshift stable. He rubbed his mount down with straw and left him with Starlight munching hay.

Rosalind had opened a shutter and was staring out at the rain when he entered. She quickly closed the shutter and ran to him.

'I fear we must remain here until the rain eases, if it does,' he added ruefully.

She pressed herself against him, entwining her arms around his waist.

'I don't mind if we have to stay here until the morrow,' she whispered.

A light entered his eyes, full of passionate promise as he raised her head and kissed her lips. No words were needed for a long time. Later, Francis managed to get a spark going with some twigs and sticks of wood he'd found in a hut in the yard. Before long the fire was blazing, filling the room with cosy warmth.

'I wish we could stay here, until this wretched war is over, Francis,' she remarked as they shared the bread, cheese and wine Francis had brought in from his saddlebag.

'So do I, my love, but nothing will separate us now.'

There was so much she wanted to know.

'Why did you act so cold towards me, after you returned from Naseby? I was so confused and unhappy.'

Francis placed his arm around her shoulder and drew her close.

'I treated you in a manner which was unforgivable, but I came from that carnage of a battle to hear I was to be promoted to colonel, making me realise that with the higher rank came greater responsibility. I wanted to do well so that I could maintain the lifestyle you are used to.'

Rosalind rested her head against his chest.

'I am not interested in the amount of wealth you can provide. I want only you, Cavalier or Roundhead. It matters not anymore.'

He kissed the top of her head.

'That evening I went to the manor to speak to Nathaniel and found him wounded. I cannot describe the torment I went through, knowing it was your brother who had done the deed. I was torn between my love for you and my loyalty to Parliament. In the end, I realised if I could make you hate me, it would make it easier to bring your brother to justice.'

She raised her head to look at him.

'Thomas did not go to the manor with the intention of killing Nathaniel,' she explained. 'There was an argument over the ownership of the estate. Nathaniel drew a dagger on Thomas. My brother retaliated in self-defence, believe me, Francis.'

'I do believe you. I knew full well what a tyrant Nathaniel Black was. It is all in the past, my dearest, and we have the rest of our lives to look forward to. A love like ours could never be destroyed by this infernal war.'

'Tell me when you first began to love me,' she asked, interlacing her fingers with his.

'I think almost from the moment I saw you, but I didn't realise it then. I was too infuriated by your haughty Royalist manner. I couldn't get you out of my mind. I knew I loved you when I kissed you at the inn, but you hold such staunch Royalist opinions, I believed it would be impossible for you to love one of the enemy.'

Rosalind rested her head against his chest again, hearing the steady thump of his heart.

'How wrong you were, my love. It was at the inn, when you kissed me, that I knew I loved you, too. We have wasted so much time, Francis, but now we can put the war behind us and begin our life together.'

Francis sighed.

'How I wish we could, but at least I think the war is drawing to a conclusion. Prince Rupert has surrendered

Bristol and perhaps the way is clear to start negotiating with the King. I am so glad we declared our love for one another before it was too late and we were parted.'

'Parted?' Rosalind echoed in alarm.

'I am to be recalled to London in the next few days, to serve General Cromwell at army headquarters. It means the days of moving from area to area, in command of a troop, are over.'

'I will not be parted from you,' she said anxiously.

'It will only be for a little while,' he assured her, 'until I can find somewhere for us to live. It would be more pleasant for you to remain at the manor for the time being. London is a crowded place, with cramped buildings almost touching across the streets and the filth and stench are appalling. You would be unhappy living there after being here in Sussex.'

'I would miss my home, but my place is with you. We have had no life together yet and I don't wish to be parted from you now.'

Francis gazed at her with love and tenderness in his eyes.

'Then we never will be parted, if that is your wish. Let us hope this war will be over soon and the conflict can be settled around a table and not on any more battlefields.'

Rosalind murmured her agreement, but there were still fears which plagued her.

'What will happen to Thomas when he returns to England? Will his property be restored to him?'

'I cannot answer that, Rosalind. I personally have no wish to dispossess your brother. I have my own estate at Thannet Hall in Kent. We will go to live there when the war is over. My mother will be happy to know I have married a Royalist lady.'

'I am so looking forward to meeting her, Francis.'

'She will love you as much as I do, my lovely wife.'

Rosalind laughed.

'Not quite as much, I think.'

'Shall we make ourselves comfortable until this rain eases?'

His gaze strayed to the bed and her cheeks flushed a delicate shade of pink when she saw his eyes darken with passion, enveloping her with his love. His lips met her own and in that moment she proved to him she had truly yielded all to him, basking in the wonderful feeling of being loved. Her dearest enemy had become her dearest love.

THE END

We do hope that you have enjoyed reading this large print book.

Did you know that all of our titles are available for purchase?

We publish a wide range of high quality large print books including:
Romances, Mysteries, Classics
General Fiction
Non Fiction and Westerns

Special interest titles available in large print are:
The Little Oxford Dictionary
Music Book, Song Book
Hymn Book, Service Book

Also available from us courtesy of Oxford University Press:
Young Readers' Dictionary
(large print edition)
Young Readers' Thesaurus
(large print edition)

For further information or a free brochure, please contact us at:
Ulverscroft Large Print Books Ltd.,
The Green, Bradgate Road, Anstey,
Leicester, LE7 7FU, England.
Tel: (00 44) **0116 236 4325**
Fax: (00 44) **0116 234 0205**

SUMMER IN HANOVER SQUARE

Charlotte Grey

The impoverished Margaret Lambart is suddenly flung into all the glitter of the Season in Regency London. Suspected by her godmother's nephew, the influential Marquis St. George, of being merely a common adventuress, she has, nevertheless, a brilliant success, and attracts the attentions of the young Duke of Oxford. However, when the Marquis discovers that Margaret is far from wanting a husband he finds he has to revise his estimate of her true worth.

CONFLICT OF HEARTS

Gillian Kaye

Somerset, at the end of World War I: Daniel Holley, unhappily married to an ailing wife and father of four grown-up children, is attracted to beautiful schoolteacher Harriet Bray, but he knows his love is hopeless. Daniel's only daughter, Amy, who dreams of becoming a milliner and is caught up in her love for young bank clerk John Tottle, looks on as the drama of Daniel and Harriet's fate and happiness gradually unfolds.

THE SOLDIER'S WOMAN

Freda M. Long

When Lieutenant Alain d'Albert was deserted by his girlfriend, a replacement was at hand in the shape of Christina Calvi, whose yearning for respectability through marriage did not quite coincide with her profession as a soldier's woman. Christina's obsessive love for Alain was not returned. The handsome hussar married an heiress and banished the soldier's woman from his life. But Christina was unswerving in the pursuit of her dream and Alain found his resistance weakening . . .